The Village Watch-Tower

Kate Douglas Smith Wiggin

Alpha Editions

This edition published in 2024

ISBN : 9789362991713

Design and Setting By
Alpha Editions
www.alphaedis.com
Email - info@alphaedis.com

As per information held with us this book is in Public Domain.
This book is a reproduction of an important historical work. Alpha Editions uses the best technology to reproduce historical work in the same manner it was first published to preserve its original nature. Any marks or number seen are left intentionally to preserve its true form.

Contents

THE VILLAGE WATCH-TOWER .... - 1 -
THE VILLAGE WATCH-TOWER. .... - 2 -
TOM O' THE BLUEB'RY PLAINS. .... - 14 -
THE NOONING TREE. .... - 23 -
THE FORE-ROOM RUG. .... - 39 -
A VILLAGE STRADIVARIUS. .... - 50 -
THE EVENTFUL TRIP OF THE MIDNIGHT CRY. .... - 80 -

THE VILLAGE WATCH-TOWER

Dear old apple-tree, under whose gnarled branches these stories were written, to you I dedicate the book. My head was so close to you, who can tell from whence the thoughts came? I only know that when all the other trees in the orchard were barren, there were always stories to be found under your branches, and so it is our joint book, dear apple-tree. Your pink blossoms have fallen on the page as I wrote; your ruddy fruit has dropped into my lap; the sunshine streamed through your leaves and tipped my pencil with gold. The birds singing in your boughs may have lent a sweet note here and there; and do you remember the day when the gentle shower came? We just curled the closer, and you and I and the sky all cried together while we wrote "The Fore-Room Rug."

It should be a lovely book, dear apple-tree, but alas! it is not altogether that, because I am not so simple as you, and because I have strayed farther away from the heart of Mother Nature.

KATE DOUGLAS WIGGIN

"Quillcote," Hollis, Maine, August 12, 1895.

THE VILLAGE WATCH-TOWER.

It stood on the gentle slope of a hill, the old gray house, with its weather-beaten clapboards and its roof of ragged shingles. It was in the very lap of the road, so that the stage-driver could almost knock on the window pane without getting down from his seat, on those rare occasions when he brought "old Mis' Bascom" a parcel from Saco.

Humble and dilapidated as it was, it was almost beautiful in the springtime, when the dandelion-dotted turf grew close to the great stone steps; or in the summer, when the famous Bascom elm cast its graceful shadow over the front door. The elm, indeed, was the only object that ever did cast its shadow there. Lucinda Bascom said her "front door 'n' entry never hed ben used except for fun'rals, 'n' she was goin' to keep it nice for that purpose, 'n' not get it all tracked up."

She was sitting now where she had sat for thirty years. Her high-backed rocker, with its cushion of copperplate patch and its crocheted tidy, stood always by a southern window that looked out on the river. The river was a sheet of crystal, as it poured over the dam; a rushing, roaring torrent of foaming white, as it swept under the bridge and fought its way between the rocky cliffs beyond, sweeping swirling, eddying, in its narrow channel, pulsing restlessly into the ragged fissures of its shores, and leaping with a tempestuous roar into the Witches' Eel-pot, a deep wooded gorge cleft in the very heart of the granite bank.

But Lucinda Bascom could see more than the river from her favorite window. It was a much-traveled road, the road that ran past the house on its way from Liberty Village to Milliken's Mills. A tottering old sign-board, on a verdant triangle of turf, directed you over Deacon Chute's hill to the "Flag Medder Road," and from thence to Liberty Centre; the little post-office and store, where the stage stopped twice a day, was quite within eyeshot; so were the public watering-trough, Brigadier Hill, and, behind the ruins of an old mill, the wooded path that led to the Witches' Eel-pot, a favorite walk for village lovers. This was all on her side of the river. As for the bridge which knit together the two tiny villages, nobody could pass over that without being seen from the Bascoms'. The rumble of wheels generally brought a family party to the window,—Jot Bascom's wife (she that was Diadema Dennett), Jot himself, if he were in the house, little Jot, and grandpa Bascom, who looked at the passers-by with a vacant smile parting his thin lips. Old Mrs. Bascom herself did not need the rumble of wheels to tell her that a vehicle was coming, for she could see it fully ten minutes before it reached the bridge,—at the very moment it appeared at the crest of Saco Hill, where strangers pulled up their horses, on a clear day, and paused to look at Mount

Washington, miles away in the distance. Tory Hill and Saco Hill met at the bridge, and just there, too, the river road began its shady course along the east side of the stream: in view of all which "old Mis' Bascom's settin'-room winder" might well be called the "Village Watch-Tower," when you consider further that she had moved only from her high-backed rocker to her bed, and from her bed to her rocker, for more than thirty years,—ever since that july day when her husband had had a sun-stroke while painting the meeting-house steeple, and her baby Jonathan had been thereby hastened into a world not in the least ready to receive him.

She could not have lived without that window, she would have told you, nor without the river, which had lulled her to sleep ever since she could remember. It was in the south chamber upstairs that she had been born. Her mother had lain there and listened to the swirl of the water, in that year when the river was higher than the oldest inhabitant had ever seen it,—the year when the covered bridge at the Mills had been carried away, and when the one at the Falls was in hourly danger of succumbing to the force of the freshet.

All the men in both villages were working on the river, strengthening the dam, bracing the bridge, and breaking the jams of logs; and with the parting of the boom, the snapping of the bridge timbers, the crashing of the logs against the rocks, and the shouts of the river-drivers, the little Lucinda had come into the world. Some one had gone for the father, and had found him on the river, where he had been since day-break, drenched with the storm, blown fro his dangerous footing time after time, but still battling with the great heaped-up masses of logs, wrenching them from one another's grasp, and sending them down the swollen stream.

Finally the jam broke; and a cheer of triumph burst from the excited men, as the logs, freed from their bondage, swept down the raging flood, on and ever on in joyous liberty, faster and faster, till they encountered some new obstacle, when they heaped themselves together again, like puppets of Fate, and were beaten by the waves into another helpless surrender.

With the breaking of the jam, one dead monarch of the forest leaped into the air as if it had been shot from a cannon's mouth, and lodged between two jutting peaks of rock high on the river bank. Presently another log was dashed against it, but rolled off and hurried down the stream; then another, and still another; but no force seemed enough to drive the giant from its intrenched position.

"Hurry on down to the next jam, Raish, and let it alone," cried the men. "Mebbe it'll git washed off in the night, and anyhow you can't budge it with no kind of a tool we've got here."

Then from the shore came a boy's voice calling, "There's a baby up to your house!" And the men repeated in stentorian tones, "Baby up to your house, Raish! Leggo the log; you're wanted!"

"Boy or girl?" shouted the young father.

"Girl!" came back the answer above the roar of the river.

Whereupon Raish Dunnell steadied himself with his pick and taking a hatchet from his belt, cut a rude letter "L" on the side of the stranded log.

"L's for Lucindy," he laughed. "Now you log if you git's fur as Saco, drop in to my wife's folks and tell 'em the baby's name."

There had not been such a freshet for years before, and there had never been one since; so, as the quiet seasons went by, "Lucindy's log" was left in peace, the columbines blooming all about it, the harebells hanging their heads of delicate blue among the rocks that held it in place, the birds building their nests in the knot-holes of its withered side.

Seventy years had passed, and on each birthday, from the time when she was only "Raish Dunnell's little Lou," to the years when she was Lucinda Bascom, wife and mother, she had wandered down by the river side, and gazed, a little superstitiously perhaps, on the log that had been marked with an "L" on the morning she was born. It had stood the wear and tear of the elements bravely, but now it was beginning, like Lucinda, to show its age. Its back was bent, like hers; its face was seamed and wrinkled, like her own; and the village lovers who looked at it from the opposite bank wondered if, after all, it would hold out as long as "old Mis' Bascom."

She held out bravely, old Mrs. Bascom, though she was "all skin, bones, and tongue," as the neighbors said; for nobody needed to go into the Bascoms' to brighten up aunt Lucinda a bit, or take her the news; one went in to get a bit of brightness, and to hear the news.

"I should get lonesome, I s'pose," she was wont to say, "if it wa'n't for the way this house is set, and this chair, and this winder, 'n' all. Men folks used to build some o' the houses up in a lane, or turn 'em back or side to the road, so the women folks couldn't see anythin' to keep their minds off their churnin' or dish-washin'; but Aaron Dunnell hed somethin' else to think about, 'n' that was himself, first, last, and all the time. His store was down to bottom of the hill, 'n' when he come up to his meals, he used to set where he could see the door; 'n' if any cust'mer come, he could call to 'em to wait a spell till he got through eatin'. Land! I can hear him now, yellin' to 'em, with his mouth full of victuals! They hed to wait till he got good 'n' ready, too. There wa'n't so much comp'tition in business then as there is now, or he'd 'a' hed to give up eatin' or hire a clerk. ... I've always felt to be thankful that the house was on this rise o' ground. The teams hev to slow up on 'count o' the hill, 'n' it gives me consid'ble chance to see folks 'n' what they've got in the back of the wagon, 'n' one thing 'n' other. ... The neighbors is continually comin' in here to talk about things that's goin' on in the village. I like to hear 'em, but land! they can't tell me nothing'! They often say, 'For massy sakes, Lucindy Bascom, how d' you know that?' 'Why,' says I to them, 'I don't ask no questions, 'n' folks don't tell me no lies; I just set in my winder, 'n' put two 'n' two together,—that's all I do.' I ain't never ben in a playhouse, but I don't suppose the play-actors git down off the platform on t' the main floor to explain to the folks what they've ben doin', do they? I expect, if folks can't understand their draymas when the're actin' of 'em out, they have to go ignorant, don't they? Well, what do I want with explainin', when everythin' is acted out right in the road?"

There was quite a gathering of neighbors at the Bascoms' on this particular July afternoon. No invitations had been sent out, and none were needed. A common excitement had made it vital that people should drop in somewhere, and speculate about certain interesting matters well known to be going on in the community, but going on in such an underhand and secretive fashion that it well-nigh destroyed one's faith in human nature.

The sitting-room door was open into the entry, so that whatever breeze there was might come in, and an unusual glimpse of the new foreroom rug was afforded the spectators. Everything was as neat as wax, for Diadema was a housekeeper of the type fast passing away. The great coal stove was enveloped in its usual summer wrapper of purple calico, which, tied neatly about its ebony neck and portly waist, gave it the appearance of a buxom colored lady presiding over the assembly. The kerosene lamps stood in a row on the high, narrow mantelpiece, each chimney protected from the flies by a brown paper bag inverted over its head. Two plaster Samuels praying under the pink mosquito netting adorned the ends of the shelf. There were screens at all the windows, and Diadema fidgeted nervously when a visitor came in the mosquito netting door, for fear a fly should sneak in with her.

On the wall were certificates of membership in the Missionary Society; a picture of Maidens welcoming Washington in the Streets of Alexandria, in a frame of cucumber seeds; and an interesting document setting forth the claims of the Dunnell family as old settlers long before the separation of Maine from Massachusetts,—the fact bein' established by an obituary notice reading, "In Saco, December 1791, Dorcas, daughter of Abiathar Dunnell, two months old of Fits unbaptized."

"He may be goin' to marry Eunice, and he may not," observed Almira Berry; "though what she wants of Reuben Hobson is more 'n I can make out. I never see a widower straighten up as he has this last year. I guess he's been lookin' round pretty lively, but couldn't find anybody that was fool enough to give him any encouragement."

"Mebbe she wants to get married," said Hannah Sophia, in a tone that spoke volumes. "When Parson Perkins come to this parish, one of his first calls was on Eunice Emery. He always talked like the book o' Revelation; so says he, 'have you got your weddin' garment on, Miss Emery?' says he. 'No,' says she, 'but I ben tryin' to these twenty years.' She was always full of her jokes, Eunice was!"

"The Emerys was always a humorous family," remarked Diadema, as she annihilated a fly with a newspaper. "Old Silas Emery was an awful humorous man. He used to live up on the island; and there come a freshet one year, and he said he got his sofy 'n' chairs off, anyhow!" That was just his jokin'. He hadn't a sign of a sofy in the house; 't was his wife Sophy he meant, she that was Sophy Swett. Then another time, when I was a little mite of a thin runnin' in 'n' out o' his yard, he caught holt o' me, and says he, 'You'd better take care, sissy; when I kill you and two more, thet'll be three children I've killed!' Land! you couldn't drag me inside that yard for years afterwards. ... There! she's got a fire in the cook-stove; there's a stream o' smoke comin' out o' the kitchen chimbley. I'm willin' to bet my new rug she's goin' to be married tonight!'

"Mebbe she's makin' jell'," suggested Hannah Sophia.

"Jell'!" ejaculated Mrs. Jot scornfully. "Do you s'pose Eunice Emery would build up a fire in the middle o' the afternoon 'n' go to makin' a jell', this hot day? Besides, there ain't a currant gone into her house this week, as I happen to know."

"It's a dretful thick year for fol'age," mumbled grandpa Bascom, appearing in the door with his vacant smile. "I declare some o' the maples looks like balls in the air."

"That's the twentieth time he's hed that over since mornin'," said Diadema. "Here, father, take your hat off 'n' set in the kitchen door 'n' shell me this mess o' peas. Now think smart, 'n' put the pods in the basket 'n' the peas in the pan; don't you mix 'em."

The old man hung his hat on the back of the chair, took the pan in his trembling hands, and began aimlessly to open the pods, while he chuckled at the hens that gathered round the doorstep when they heard the peas rattling in the pan.

"Reuben needs a wife bad enough, if that's all," remarked the Widow Buzzell, as one who had given the matter some consideration.

"I should think he did," rejoined old Mrs. Bascom. "Those children 'bout git their livin' off the road in summer, from the time the dand'lion greens is ready for diggin' till the blackb'ries 'n' choke-cherries is gone. Diademy calls 'em in 'n' gives 'em a cooky every time they go past, 'n' they eat as if they was famished. Rube Hobson never was any kind of a perviner, 'n' he's consid'able snug besides."

"He ain't goin' to better himself much," said Almira. "Eunice Emery ain't fit to housekeep for a cat. The pie she took to the pie supper at the church was so tough that even Deacon Dyer couldn't eat it; and the boys got holt of her doughnuts, and declared they was goin' fishin' next day 'n' use 'em for sinkers. She lives from hand to mouth Eunice Emery does. She's about as much of a doshy as Rube is. She'll make tea that's strong enough to bear up an egg, most, and eat her doughnuts with it three times a day rather than take the trouble to walk out to the meat or the fish cart. I know for a fact she don't make riz bread once a year."

"Mebbe her folks likes buttermilk bread best; some do," said the Widow Buzzell. "My husband always said, give him buttermilk bread to work on. He used to say my riz bread was so light he'd hev to tread on it to keep it anywheres; but when you'd eat buttermilk bread he said you'd got somethin' that stayed by you; you knew where it was every time. ... For massy sake! there's the stage stoppin' at the Hobson's door. I wonder if Rube's first wife's mother has come from Moderation? If 't is, they must 'a' made up their quarrel, for there was a time she wouldn't step foot over that doorsill. She must be goin' to stay some time, for there's a trunk on the back o' the stage. ... No, there ain't nobody gettin' out. Land, Hannah Sophia, don't push me clean through the glass! It beats me why they make winders so small that three people can't look out of 'em without crowdin'. Ain't that a wash-boiler he's handin' down? Well, it's a mercy; he's ben borrowin' long enough!"

"What goes on after dark I ain't responsible for," commented old Mrs. Bascom, "but no new wash-boiler has gone into Rube Hobson's door in the daytime for many a year, and I'll be bound it means somethin'. There goes a broom, too. Much sweepin' he'll get out o' Eunice; it's a slick 'n' a promise with her!"

"When did you begin to suspicion this, Diademy?" asked Almira Berry. "I've got as much faculty as the next one, but anybody that lives on the river road has just got to give up knowin' anything. You can't keep runnin' to the store every day, and if you could you don't find out much nowadays. Bill Peters don't take no more interest in his neighbors than a cow does in election."

"I can't get mother Bascom to see it as I do," said Diadema, "but for one thing she's ben carryin' home bundles 'bout every other night for a month, though she's ben too smart to buy anythin' here at this store. She had

Packard's horse to go to Saco last week. When she got home, jest at dusk, she drove int' the barn, 'n' bimeby Pitt Packard come to git his horse,—'t was her own buggy she went with. She looked over here when she went int' the house, 'n' she ketched my eye, though 't was half a mile away, so she never took a thing in with her, but soon as't was dark she made three trips out to the barn with a lantern, 'n' any fool could tell 't her arms was full o' pa'cels by the way she carried the lantern. The Hobsons and the Emerys have married one another more 'n once, as fur as that goes. I declare if I was goin' to get married I should want to be relation to somebody besides my own folks."

"The reason I can hardly credit it," said Hannah Sophia, "is because Eunice never had a beau in her life, that I can remember of. Cyse Higgins set up with her for a spell, but it never amounted to nothin'. It seems queer, too, for she was always so fond o' seein' men folks round that when Pitt Packard was shinglin' her barn she used to go out nights 'n' rip some o' the shingles off, so 't he'd hev more days' work on it."

"I always said 't was she that begun on Rube Hobson, not him on her," remarked the Widow Buzzell. "Their land joinin' made courtin' come dretful handy. His critters used to git in her field 'bout every other day (I always suspicioned she broke the fence down herself), and then she'd hev to go over and git him to drive 'em out. She's wed his onion bed for him two summers, as I happen to know, for I've been ou' doors more 'n common this summer, tryin' to fetch my constitution up. Diademy, don't you want to look out the back way 'n' see if Rube's come home yet?"

"He ain't," said old Mrs. Bascom, "so you needn't look; can't you see the curtains is all down? He's gone up to the Mills, 'n' it's my opinion he's gone to speak to the minister."

"He hed somethin' in the back o' the wagon covered up with an old linen lap robe; 't ain't at all likely he 'd 'a' hed that if he'd ben goin' to the minister's," objected Mrs. Jot.

"Anybody'd think you was born yesterday, to hear you talk, Diademy," retorted her mother-in-law. "When you 've set in one spot's long's I hev, p'raps you'll hev the use o' your faculties! Men folks has more 'n one way o' gettin' married, 'specially when they 're ashamed of it. ... Well, I vow, there's the little Hobson girls comin' out o' the door this minute, 'n' they 're all dressed up, and Mote don't seem to be with 'em."

Every woman in the room rose to her feet, and Diadema removed her murderous eye from a fly which she had been endeavoring to locate for some moments.

"I guess they 're goin' up to the church to meet their father 'n' Eunice, poor little things," ventured the Widow Buzzell.

"P'raps they be," said old Mrs. Bascom sarcastically; "p'raps they be goin' to church, takin' a three-quart tin pail 'n' a brown paper bundle along with 'em. ... They 're comin' over the bridge, just as I s'posed. ... Now, if they come past this house, you head 'em off, Almiry, 'n' see if you can git some satisfaction out of 'em. ... They ain't hardly old enough to hold their tongues."

An exciting interview soon took place in the middle of the road, and Almira reentered the room with the expression of one who had penetrated the inscrutable and solved the riddle of the Sphinx. She had been vouch-safed one of those gleams of light in darkness which almost dazzle the beholder.

"That's about the confirmingest thing I've heern yet!" she ejaculated, as she took off her shaker bonnet. "They say they're goin' up to their aunt Hitty's to stay two days. They're dressed in their best, clean to the skin, for I looked; 'n' it's their night gownds they've got in the bundle. They say little Mote has gone to Union to stop all night with his uncle Abijah, 'n' that leaves Rube all alone, for the smith girl that does his chores is home sick with the hives. And what do you s'pose is in the pail? *Fruit cake*,—that's what 't is, no more 'n' no less! I knowed that Smith girl didn't bake it, 'n' so I asked 'em, 'n' they said Miss Emery give it to 'em. There was two little round try-cakes, baked in muffin-rings. Eunice hed took some o' the batter out of a big loaf 'n' baked it to se how it was goin' to turn out. That means wedding-cake, or I'm mistaken!"

"There ain't no gittin' round that," agreed the assembled company, "now is there, Mis' Bascom?"

Old Mrs. Bascom wet her finger, smoothed the parting of her false front, and looked inscrutable.

"I don't see why you're so secret," objected Diadema.

"I've got my opinions, and I've had 'em some time," observed the good lady. "I don't know 's I'm bound to tell 'em and have 'em held up to ridicule. Let the veal hang, I say. If any one of us is right, we'll all know to-morrow."

"Well, all any of us has got to judge from is appearances," said Diadema, "and how you can twist 'em one way, and us another, stumps me!"

"Perhaps I see more appearances than you do," retorted her mother-in-law. "Some folks mistakes all they see for all there is. I was reading a detective story last week. It seems there was an awful murder in Schenectady, and a mother and her two children was found dead in one bed, with bullet holes in their heads. The husband was away on business, and there wasn't any near neighbors to hear her screech. Well, the detectives come from far and from near, and begun to work up the case. One of 'em thought 't was the husband,—though he set such store by his wife he went ravin' crazy when he heard she was dead,—one of 'em laid it on the children,—though they was both under six years old; and one decided it was suicide,—though the woman was a church member and didn't know how to fire a gun off, besides. And then there come along a detective younger and smarter than all the rest, and says he, 'If all you bats have seen everything you can see, I guess I'll take a look around,' says he. Sure enough, there was a rug with 'Welcome' on it layin' in front of the washstand, and when he turned it up he found an elegant diamond stud with a man's full name and address on the gold part. He took a train and went right to the man's house. He was so taken by surprise (he hadn't missed the stud, for he had a full set of 'em) that he owned right up and confessed the murder."

"I don't see as that's got anything to do with this case," said Diadema.

"It's got this much to do with it," replied old Mrs. Bascom, "that perhaps you've looked all round the room and seen everything you had eyes to see, and perhaps I've had wit enough to turn up the rug in front o' the washstand."

"Whoever he marries now, Mis' Bascom'll have to say 't was the one she meant," laughed the Widow Buzzell.

"I never was caught cheatin' yet, and if I live till Saturday I shall be seventy-one years old," said the old lady with some heat. "Hand me Jot's lead pencil, Diademy, and that old envelope on the winder sill. I'll write the name I think of, and shut it up in the old Bible. My hand's so stiff to-day I can't hardly move it, but I guess I can make it plain enough to satisfy you."

"That's fair 'n' square," said Hannah Sophia, "and for my pat I hope it ain't Eunice, for I like her too well. What they're goin' to live on is more 'n I can see. Add nothin' to nothin' 'n' you git nothin',—that's arethmetic! He ain't hed a cent o' ready money sence he failed up four years ago, 'thout it was that hundred dollars that fell to him from his wife's aunt. Eunice'll hev her hands full this winter, I guess, with them three hearty children 'n' him all wheezed up with phthisic from October to April!... Who's that coming' down Tory Hill? It's Rube's horse 'n' Rube's wagon, but it don't look like Rube."

"Yes, it's Rube; but he's got a new Panama hat, 'n' he 's hed his linen duster washed," said old Mrs. Bascom. ... "Now, do you mean to tell me that that woman with a stuck-up hat on is Eunice Emery? It ain't, 'n' that green parasol don't belong to this village. He's drivin' her into his yard!... Just as I s'posed, it's that little, smirkin' worthless school-teacher up to the Mills.—Don't break my neck, Diademy; can't you see out the other winder?—Yes, he's helpin' her out, 'n' showin' her in. He can't 'a' ben married more'n ten minutes, for he's goin' clear up the steps to open the door for her!"

"Wait 'n' see if he takes his horse out," said Hannah Sophia. "Mebbe he'll drive her back in a few minutes. ... No, he's onhitched! ... There, he's hangin' up the head-stall!"

"I've ben up in the attic chamber," called the Widow Buzzell, as she descended the stairs; "she's pulled up the curtains, and took off her hat right in front o' the winder, 's bold as a brass kettle! She's come to stay! Ain't that Rube Hobson all over,—to bring another woman int' this village 'stid o' weedin' one of 'em out as he'd oughter. He ain't got any more public sperit than a—hedgehog, 'n' never had!"

Almira drew on her mitts excitedly, tied on her shaker, and started for the door.

"I'm goin' over to Eunice's," she said, "and I'm goin' to take my bottle of camphire. I shouldn't wonder a mite if I found her in a dead faint on the kitchen floor. Nobody need tell me she wa'n't buildin' hopes."

"I'll go with you," said the Widow Buzzell. "I'd like to see with my own eyes how she takes it, 'n' it'll be too late to tell if I wait till after supper. If she'd ben more open with me 'n' ever asked for my advice, I could 'a' told her it wa'n't the first time Rube Hobson has played that trick."

"I'd come too if 't wa'n't milkin' but Jot ain't home from the Centre, and I've got to do his chores; come in as you go along back, will you?" asked Diadema.

Hannah Sophia remained behind, promising to meet them at the post-office and hear the news. As the two women walked down the hill she drew the old envelope from the Bible and read the wavering words scrawled upon it in old Mrs. Bascom's rheumatic and uncertain hand,—

the milikins Mills Teecher.

"Well Lucindy, you do make good use o' your winder," she exclaimed, "but how you pitched on anything so onlikely as her is more'n I can see."

"Just because 't was onlikely. A man's a great sight likelier to do an onlikely thing than he is a likely one, when it comes to marryin'. In the first place, Rube sent his children to school up to the Mills 'stid of to the brick schoolhouse, though he had to pay a little something to get 'em taken in to another deestrick. They used to come down at night with their hands full o' 'ward o' merit cards. Do you s'pose I thought they got 'em for good behavior, or for knowin' their lessons? Then aunt Hitty told me some question or other Rube had asked examination day. Since when has Rube Hobson 'tended examinations, thinks I. And when I see the girl, a red-and-white paper doll that wouldn't know whether to move the churn-dasher up 'n' down or round 'n' round, I made up my mind that bein' a man he'd take her for certain, and not his next-door neighbor of a sensible age and a house 'n' farm 'n' cow 'n' buggy!"

"Sure enough," agreed Hannah Sophia, "though that don't account for Eunice's queer actions, 'n' the pa'cels 'n' the fruit cake."

"When I make out a case," observed Mrs. Bascom modestly, "I ain't one to leave weak spots in it. If I guess at all, I go all over the ground 'n' stop when I git through. Now, sisters or no sisters, Maryabby Emery ain't spoke to Eunice sence she moved to Salem. But if Eunice has ben bringin' pa'cels home, Maryabby must 'a' paid for what was in 'em; and if she's ben bakin' fruit cake this hot day, why Maryabby used to be so font o' fruit cake her folks were afraid she'd have fits 'n' die. I shall be watchin' here as usual tomorrow mornin', 'n' if Maryabby don't drive int' Eunice's yard before noon I won't brag any more for a year to come."

Hannah Sophia gazed at old Mrs. Bascom with unstinted admiration. "You do beat all," she said; "and I wish I could stay all night 'n' see how it turns out, but Almiry is just comin' over the bridge, 'n' I must start 'n' meet her. Good-by. I'm glad to see you so smart; you always look slim, but I guess you'll tough it out's long 's the rest of us. I see your log was all right, last time I was down side o' the river."

"They say it 's jest goin' to break in two in the middle, and fall into the river," cheerfully responded Lucinda. "They say it's just hanging' on by a thread. Well, that's what they 've ben sayin' about me these ten years, 'n' here I be still hanging! It don't make no odds, I guess, whether it's a thread or a rope you 're hangin' by, so long as you hang."

* * *

The next morning, little Mote Hobson, who had stayed all night with his uncle in Union, was walking home by the side of the river. He strolled along, the happy, tousle-headed, barefooted youngster, eyes one moment on the trees in the hope of squirrels and birds'-nests, the next on the ground in search of the first blueberries. As he stooped to pick up a bit of shining quartz to add to the collection in his ragged trousers' pockets he glanced across the river, and at that very instant Lucinda's log broke gently in twain, rolled down the bank, crumbling as it went, and, dropping in like a tired child, was carried peacefully along on the river's breast.

Mote walked more quickly after that. It was quite a feather in his cap to see, with his own eyes, the old landmark slip from its accustomed place and float down the stream. The other boys would miss it and say, "It's gone!" He would say, "I saw it go!"

Grandpa Bascom was standing at the top of the hill. His white locks were uncovered, and he was in his shirt-sleeves. Baby Jot, as usual, held fast by his shaking hand, for they loved each other, these two. The cruel stroke of the sun that had blurred the old man's brain had spared a blessed something in him that won the healing love of children.

"How d' ye, Mote?" he piped in his feeble voice. "They say Lucindy's dead. ... Jot says she is, 'n' Diademy says she is, 'n' I guess she is. ... It 's a dretful thick year for fol'age; ... some o' the maples looks like balls in the air."

Mote looked in at the window. The neighbors were hurrying to and fro. Diadema sat with her calico apron up to her face, sobbing; and for the first morning in thirty years, old Mrs. Bascom's high-backed rocker was empty, and there was no one sitting in the village watch-tower.

TOM O' THE BLUEB'RY PLAINS.

The sky is a shadowless blue; the noon-day sun glows fiercely; a cloud of dust rises from the burning road whenever the hot breeze stirs the air, or whenever a farm wagon creaks along, its wheels sinking into the deep sand.

In the distance, where the green of the earth joins the blue of the sky, gleams the silver line of a river.

As far as the eye an reach, the ground is covered with blueberry bushes; red leaves peeping among green ones; bloom of blue fruit hanging in full warm clusters,—spheres of velvet mellowed by summer sun, moistened with crystal dew, spiced with fragrance of woods.

In among the blueberry bushes grow huckleberries, "choky pears," and black-snaps.

Gnarled oaks and stunted pines lift themselves out of the wilderness of shrubs. They look dwarfed and gloomy, as if Nature had been an untender mother, and denied them proper nourishment.

The road is a little-traveled one, and furrows of feathery grasses grow between the long, hot, sandy stretches of the wheel-ruts.

The first goldenrod gleams among the loose stones at the foot of the alder bushes. Whole families of pale butterflies, just out of their long sleep, perch on the brilliant stalks and tilter up and down in the sunshine.

Straggling processions of wooly brown caterpillars wend their way in the short grass by the wayside, where the wild carrot and the purple bull-thistle are coming into bloom.

The song of birds is seldom heard, and the blueberry plains are given over to silence save for the buzzing of gorged flies, the humming of bees, and the chirping of crickets that stir the drowsy air when the summer begins to wane.

It is so still that the shuffle-shuffle of a footstep can be heard in the distance, the tinkle of a tin pail swinging musically to and fro, the swish of an alder switch cropping the heads of the roadside weeds. All at once a voice breaks the stillness. Is it a child's, a woman's, or a man's? Neither yet all three.

"I'd much d'ruth-er walk in the bloom-in' gy-ar-ding,

An' hear the whis-sle of the jol-ly

—swain."

Everybody knows the song, and everybody knows the cracked voice. The master of this bit of silent wilderness is coming home: it is Tom o' the blueb'ry plains.

He is more than common tall, with a sandy beard, and a mop of tangled hair straggling beneath his torn straw hat. A square of wet calico drips from under the back of the hat. His gingham shirt is open at the throat, showing his tanned neck and chest. Warm as it is, he wears portions of at least three coats on his back. His high boots, split in foot and leg, are mended and spliced and laced and tied on with bits of shingle rope. He carries a small tin pail of molasses. It has a bail of rope, and a battered cover with a knob of sticky newspaper. Over one shoulder, suspended on a crooked branch, hangs a bundle of basket stuff,—split willow withes and the like; over the other swings a decrepit, bottomless, three-legged chair.

I call him the master of the plains, but in faith he had no legal claim to the title. If he owned a habitation or had established a home on any spot in the universe, it was because no man envied him what he took; for Tom was one of God's fools, a foot-loose pilgrim in this world of ours, a poor addle-pated, simple-minded, harmless creature,—in village parlance, a "softy."

Mother or father, sister or brother, he had none, nor ever had, so far as any one knew; but how should people who had to work from sun-up to candlelight to get the better of the climate have leisure to discover whether or no Blueb'ry Tom had any kin?

At some period in an almost forgotten past there had been a house on Tom's particular patch of the plains. It had long since tumbled into ruins and served for fire-wood and even the chimney bricks had disappeared one by one, as the monotonous seasons came and went.

Tom had settled himself in an old tool-shop, corn-house, or rude out-building of some sort that had belonged to the ruined cottage. Here he had set up his house-hold gods; and since no one else had ever wanted a home in this dreary tangle of berry bushes, where the only shade came from stunted pines that flung shriveled arms to the sky and dropped dead cones to the sterile earth, here he remained unmolested.

In the lower part of the hut he kept his basket stuff and his collection of two-legged and three-legged chairs. In the course of evolution they never sprouted another leg, those chairs; as they were given to him, so they remained. The upper floor served for his living-room, and was reached by a ladder from the ground, for there was no stairway inside.

No one had ever been in the little upper chamber. When a passer-by chanced to be-think him that Tom's hermitage was close at hand, he sometimes turned in his team by a certain clump of white birches and drove nearer to the house, intending to remind Tom that there was a chair to willow-bottom the next time he came to the village. But at the noise of the wheels Tom drew in his ladder; and when the visitor alighted and came within sight, it was to find the inhospitable host standing in the opening of the second-story window, a quaint figure framed in green branches, the ladder behind him, and on his face a kind of impenetrable dignity, as he shook his head and said, "Tom ain't ter hum; Tom's gone to Bonny Eagle."

There was something impressive about his way of repelling callers; it was as effectual as a door slammed in the face, and yet there was a sort of mendacious courtesy about it. No one ever cared to go further; and indeed there was no mystery to tempt the curious, and no spoil to attract the mischievous or the malicious. Any one could see, without entering, the straw bed in the far corner, the beams piled deep with red and white oak acorns, the strings of dried apples and bunches of everlastings hanging from the rafters, and the half-finished baskets filled with blown bird's-eggs, pine cones, and pebbles.

No home in the village was better loved than Tom's retreat in the blueberry plains. Whenever he approached it, after a long day's tramp, when he caught the first sight of the white birches that marked the gateway to his estate and showed him where to turn off the public road into his own private grounds, he smiled a broader smile than usual, and broke into his well-known song:

"I'd much d'ruth-er walk in the bloom-in' gy-ar-ding,

An' hear the whis-sle of the jol-ly

—swain."

Poor Tom could never catch the last note. He had sung the song for more than forty years, but the memory of this tone was so blurred, and his cherished ideal of it so high (or so low, rather), that he never managed to reach it.

Oh, if only summer were eternal! Who could wish a better supper than ripe berries and molasses? Nor was there need of sleeping under roof nor of lighting candles to grope his way to pallet of straw, when he might have the blue vault of heaven arching over him, and all God's stars for lamps, and for a bed a horse blanket stretched over an elastic couch of pine needles. There were two gaunt pines that had been dropping their polished spills for centuries, perhaps silently adding, year by year, another layer of aromatic springiness to poor Tom's bed. Flinging his tired body on this grateful couch, burying his head in the crushed sweet fern of his pillow with one deep-drawn sigh of pleasure,—there, haunted by no past and harassed by no future, slept God's fool as sweetly as a child.

Yes, if only summer were eternal, and youth as well!

But when the blueberries had ripened summer after summer, and the gaunt pine-trees had gone on for many years weaving poor Tom's mattress, there came a change in the aspect of things. He still made his way to the village, seeking chairs to mend; but he was even more unkempt than of old, his tall figure was bent, and his fingers trembled as he wove the willow strands in and out, and over and under.

There was little work to do, moreover, for the village had altogether retired from business, and was no longer in competition with its neighbors: the dam was torn away, the sawmills were pulled down; husbands and fathers were laid in the churchyard, sons and brothers and lovers had gone West, and mothers and widows and spinsters stayed on, each in her quiet house alone. "'T ain't no hardship when you get used to it," said the Widow Buzzell. "Land sakes! a lantern 's 's good 's a man any time, if you only think so, 'n' 't ain't half so much trouble to keep it filled up!"

But Tom still sold a basket occasionally, and the children always gathered about him for the sake of hearing him repeat his well-worn formula,—"Tom allers puts two handles on baskets: one to take 'em up by, one to set 'em down by." This was said with a beaming smile and a wise shake of the head, as if he were announcing a great discovery to an expectant world. And then he would lay down his burden of basket stuff, and, sitting under an apple-tree in somebody's side yard, begin his task of willow-bottoming an old chair. It was a pretty sight enough, if one could keep back the tears,—the kindly, simple fellow with the circle of children about his knees. Never a village fool without a troop of babies at his heels. They love him, too, till we teach them to mock.

When he was younger, he would sing,

"*Rock-a-by, baby, on the treetop,*"

and dance the while, swinging his unfinished basket to and fro for a cradle. He was too stiff in the joints for dancing nowadays, but he still sang the "bloomin' gy-ar-ding" when ever they asked him, particularly if some apple-cheeked little maid would say, "Please, Tom!" He always laughed then, and, patting the child's hand, said, "Pooty gal,—got eyes!" The youngsters dance with glee at this meaningless phrase, just as their mothers had danced years before when it was said to them.

Summer waned. In the moist places the gentian uncurled its blue fringes; purple asters and gay Joe Pye waved their colors by the roadside; tall primroses put their yellow bonnets on, and peeped over the brooks to see themselves; and the dusty pods of the milkweed were bursting with their silky fluffs, the spinning of the long summer. Autumn began to paint the maples red and the elms yellow, for the early days of September brought a frost. Some one remarked at the village store that old Blueb'ry Tom must not be suffered to stay on the plains another winter, now that he was getting so feeble,—not if the "*s*eleckmen" had to root him out and take him to the poor-farm. He would surely starve or freeze, and his death would be laid at their door.

Tom was interviewed. Persuasion, logic, sharp words, all failed to move him one jot or tittle. He stood in his castle door, with the ladder behind him, smiling, always smiling (none but the fool smiles always, nor always weeps), and saying to all visitors, "Tom ain't ter hum; Tom's gone to Bonny Eagle; Tom don' want to go to the poor-farm."

November came in surly.

The cheerful stir and bustle of the harvest were over, the corn was shocked, the apples and pumpkins were gathered into barns. The problem of Tom's future was finally laid before the selectmen; and since the poor fellow's mild obstinancy had defeated all attempts to conquer it, the sheriff took the matter in hand.

The blueberry plains looked bleak and bare enough now. It had rained incessantly for days, growing ever colder and colder as it rained. The sun came out at last, but it shone in a wintry sort of way,—like a duty smile,—as if light, not heat, were its object. A keen wind blew the dead leaves hither and thither in a wild dance that had no merriment in it. A blackbird flew under an old barrel by the wayside, and, ruffling himself into a ball, remarked despondently that feathers were no sort of protection in this kind of climate. A snowbird, flying by, glanced in at the barrel, and observed that anybody who minded a little breeze like that had better join the woodcocks, who were leaving for the South by the night express.

The blueberry bushes were stripped bare of green. The stunted pines and sombre hemlocks looked in tone with the landscape now; where all was dreary they did not seem amiss.

"Je-whilikins!" exclaimed the sheriff as he drew up his coat collar. "A madhouse is the place for the man who wants to live ou'doors in the winter time; the poor-farm is too good for him."

But Tom was used to privation, and even to suffering. "Ou'doors" was the only home he knew, and with all its rigors he loved it. He looked over the barren plains, knowing, in a dull sort of way, that they would shortly be covered with snow; but he had three coats, two of them with sleeves, and the crunch-crunch of the snow under his tread was music to his ears. Then, too, there were a few hospitable firesides where he could always warm himself; and the winter would soon be over, the birds would come again,—new birds, singing the old songs,—the sap would mount in the trees, the buds swell on the blueberry bushes, and the young ivory leaves push their ruddy tips through the softening ground. The plains were fatherland and mother-country, home and kindred, to Tom. He loved the earth that nourished him, and he saw through all the seeming death in nature the eternal miracle of the resurrection. To him winter was never cruel. He looked underneath her white mantle, saw the infant spring hidden in her warm bosom, and was content to wait. Content to wait? Content to starve, content to freeze, if only he need not be carried into captivity.

The poor-farm was not a bad place, either, if only Tom had been a reasonable being. To be sure, when Hannah Sophia Palmer asked old Mrs. Pinkham how she liked it, she answered, with a patient sigh, that "her 'n' Mr. Pinkham hed lived there goin' on nine year, workin' their fingers to the bone 'most, 'n' yet they hadn't been able to lay up a cent!" If this peculiarity of administration was its worst feature, it was certainly one that would have had no terrors for Tom o' the blueb'ry plains. Terrors of some sort, nevertheless, the poor-farm had for him; and when the sheriff's party turned in by the clump of white birches and approached the cabin, they found that fear had made the simple wise. Tom had provisioned the little upper chamber, and, in place of the piece of sacking that usually served him for a door in winter, he had woven a defense of willow. In fine, he had taken all his basket stuff, and, treating the opening through which he entered and left his home precisely as if it were a bottomless chair, he had filled it in solidly, weaving to and fro, by night as well as by day, till he felt, poor fool, as safely intrenched as if he were in the heart of a fortress.

The sheriff tied his horse to a tree, and Rube Hobson and Pitt Packard got out of the double wagon. Two men laughed when they saw the pathetic defense, but the other shut his lips together and caught his breath. (He had been born on a poor-farm, but no one knew it at Pleasant River.) They called Tom's name repeatedly, but no other sound broke the silence of the plains save the rustling of the wind among the dead leaves.

"Numb-head!" muttered the sheriff, pounding on the side of the cabin with his whip-stock. "Come out and show yourself! We know you're in there, and it's no use hiding!"

At last in response to a deafening blow from Rube Hobson's hard fist, there came the answering note of a weak despairing voice.

"Tom ain't ter hum," it said; "Tom's gone to Bonny Eagle."

"That's all right!" guffawed the men; "but you've got to go some more, and go a diff'rent way. It ain't no use fer you to hold back; we've got a ladder, and by Jiminy! you go with us this time!"

The ladder was put against the side of the hut, and Pitt Packard climbed up, took his jack-knife, slit the woven door from top to bottom, and turned back the flap.

The men could see the inside of the chamber now. They were humorous persons who could strain a joke to the snapping point, but they felt, at last, that there was nothing especially amusing in the situation. Tom was huddled in a heap on the straw bed in the far corner. The vacant smile had fled from his face, and he looked, for the first time in his life, quite distraught.

"Come along, Tom," said the sheriff kindly; "we're going to take you where you can sleep in a bed, and have three meals a day."

"I'd much d'ruth-er walk in the bloom-in' gy-ar-ding,"

sang Tom quaveringly, as he hid his head in a paroxysm of fear.

"Well, there ain't no bloomin' gardings to walk in jest now, so come along and be peaceable."

"Tom don' want to go to the poor-farm," he wailed piteously.

But there was no alternative. They dragged him off the bed and down the ladder as gently as possible; then Rube Hobson held him on the back seat of the wagon, while the sheriff unhitched the horse. As they were on the point of starting, the captive began to wail and struggle more than ever, the burden of his plaint being a wild and tremulous plea for his pail of molasses.

"Dry up, old softy, or I'll put the buggy robe over your head!" muttered Rube Hobson, who had not had much patience when he started on the trip, and had lost it all by this time.

"By thunder! he shall hev his molasses, if he thinks he wants it!" said Pitt Packard, and he ran up the ladder and brought it down, comforting the shivering creature thus, for he lapsed into a submissive silence that lasted until the unwelcome journey was over.

Tom remained at the poorhouse precisely twelve hours. It did not enter the minds of the authorities that any one so fortunate as to be admitted into that happy haven would decline to stay there. The unwilling guest disappeared early on the morrow of his arrival, and, after some search, they followed him to the old spot. He had climbed into his beloved retreat, and, having learned nothing from experience, had mended the willow door as best he could, and laid him down in peace. They dragged him out again, and this time more impatiently; for it was exasperating to see a man (even if he were a fool) fight against a bed and three meals a day.

The second attempt was little more successful than the first. As a place of residence, the poor-farm did not seem any more desirable or attractive on near acquaintance than it did at long range. Tom remained a week, because he was kept in close confinement; but when they judged that he was weaned from his old home, they loosed his bonds, and—back to the plains he sped, like an arrow shot from the bow, or like a bit of iron leaping to the magnet.

What should be done with him?

Public opinion was divided. Some people declared that the village had done its duty, and if the "dog-goned lunk-head" wanted to starve and freeze, it was his funeral, not theirs. Others thought that the community had no resource but to bear the responsibility of its irresponsible children, however troublesome they might be. There was entire unanimity of view so far as the main issues were concerned. It was agreed that nobody at the poor-farm had leisure to stand guard over Tom night and day, and that the sheriff could not be expected to spend his time forcing him out of his hut on the blueberry plains.

There was but one more expedient to be tried, a very simple and ingenious but radical and comprehensive one, which, in Rube Hobson's opinion, would strike at the root of the matter.

Tom had fled from captivity for the third time.

He had stolen out at daybreak, and, by an unexpected stroke of fortune, the molasses pail was hanging on a nail by the shed door. The remains of a battered old bushel basket lay on the wood-pile: bottom it had none, nor handles; rotundity of side had long since disappeared, and none but its maker would have known it for a basket. Tom caught it up in his flight, and, seizing the first crooked stick that offered, he slung the dear familiar burden over his shoulder and started off on a jog-trot.

Heaven, how happy he was! It was the rosy dawn of an Indian summer day,— a warm jewel of a day, dropped into the bleak world of yesterday without a hint of beneficent intention; one of those enchanting weather surprises with which Dame Nature reconciles us to her stern New England rule.

The joy that comes of freedom, and the freedom that comes of joy, unbent the old man's stiffened joints. He renewed his youth at every mile. He ran like a lapwing. When his feet first struck the sandy soil of the plains, he broke into old song of the "bloom-in' gy-ar-ding" and the "jolly swain," and in the marvelous mental and spiritual exhilaration born of the supreme moment he almost grasped that impossible last note. His heard could hardly hold its burden of rapture when he caught the well-known gleam of the white birches. He turned into the familiar path, boy's blood thumping in old man's veins. The past week had been a dreadful dream. A few steps more and he would be within sight, within touch of home,—home at last! No—what was wrong? He must have gone beyond it, in his reckless haste! Strange that he could have forgotten the beloved spot! Can lover mistake the way to sweetheart's window? Can child lose the path to mother's knee?

He turned,—ran hither and thither, like one distraught. A nameless dread flitted through his dull mind, chilling his warm blood, paralyzing the activity of the moment before. At last, with a sob like that of a frightened child who flies from some imagined evil lurking in darkness, he darted back to the white birches and started anew. This time he trusted to blind instinct; his feet knew the path, and, left to themselves, they took him through the tangle of dry bushes straight to his—

It had vanished!

Nothing but ashes remained to mark the spot,—nothing but ashes! And these, ere many days, the autumn winds would scatter, and the leafless branches on which they fell would shake them off lightly, never dreaming that they hid the soul of a home. Nothing but ashes!

Poor Tom o' the blueb'ry plains!

THE NOONING TREE.

The giant elm stood in the centre of the squire's fair green meadows, and was known to all the country round about as the "Bean ellum." The other trees had seemingly retired to a respectful distance, as if they were not worthy of closer intimacy; and so it stood alone, king of the meadow, monarch of the village.

It shot from the ground for a space, straight, strong, and superb, and then bust into nine splendid branches, each a tree in itself, all growing symmetrically from the parent trunk, and casting a grateful shadow under which all the inhabitants of the tiny village might have gathered.

It was not alone its size, its beauty, its symmetry, its density of foliage, that made it the glory of the neighborhood, but the low grown of its branches and the extra-ordinary breadth of its shade. Passers-by from the adjacent towns were wont to hitch their teams by the wayside, crawl through the stump fence and walk across the fields, for a nearer view of its magnificence. One man, indeed, was known to drive by the tree every day during the summer, and lift his hat to it, respectfully, each time he passed; but he was a poet and his intellect was not greatly esteemed in the village.

The elm was almost as beautiful in one season as in another. In the spring it rose from moist fields and mellow ploughed ground, its tiny brown leaf buds bursting with pride at the thought of the loveliness coiled up inside. In summer it stood in the midst of a waving garden of buttercups and whiteweed, a towering mass of verdant leafage, a shelter from the sun and a refuge from the storm; a cool, splendid, hospitable dome, under which the weary farmer might fling himself, and gaze upward as into the heights and depths of an emerald heaven. As for the birds, they made it a fashionable summer resort, the most commodious and attractive in the whole country; with no limit to the accommodations for those of a gregarious turn of mind, liking the advantages of select society combined with country air. In the autumn it held its own; for when the other elms changed their green to duller tints, the nooning tree put on a gown of yellow, and stood out against the far background of sombre pine woods a brilliant mass of gold and brown. In winter, when there was no longer dun of upturned sod, nor waving daisy gardens, nor ruddy autumn grasses, it rose above the dazzling snow crust, lifting its bare, shapely branches in sober elegance and dignity, and seeming to say, "Do not pity me; I have been, and, please God, I shall be!"

Whenever the weather was sufficiently mild, it was used as a "nooning" tree by all the men at work in the surrounding fields; but it was in haying time that it became the favorite lunching and "bangeing" place for Squire Bean's hands and those of Miss Vilda Cummins, who owned the adjoining farm.

The men congregated under the spreading branches at twelve o' the clock, and spent the noon hour there, eating and "swapping" stories, as they were doing to-day.

Each had a tin pail, and each consumed a quantity of "flour food" that kept the housewives busy at the cook stove from morning till night. A glance at Pitt Packard's luncheon, for instance, might suffice as an illustration, for, as Jabe Slocum said, "Pitt took after both his parents; one et a good deal, 'n' the other a good while." His pail contained four doughnuts, a quarter section of pie, six buttermilk biscuits, six ginger cookies, a baked cup custard, and a quart of cold coffee. This quantity was a trifle unusual, but every man in the group was lined throughout with pie, cemented with buttermilk bread, and riveted with doughnuts.

Jabe Slocum and Brad Gibson lay extended slouchingly, their cowhide boots turned up to the sky; Dave Milliken, Steve Webster, and the others leaned back against the tree-trunk, smoking clay pipes, or hugging their knees and chewing blades of grass reflectively.

One man sat apart from the rest, gloomily puffing rings of smoke into the air. After a while he lay down in the grass with his head buried in his hat, sleeping to all appearances, while the others talked and laughed; for he had no stories, though he put in an absent-minded word or two when he was directly addressed. This was the man from Tennessee, Matt Henderson, dubbed "Dixie" for short. He was a giant fellow,—a "great gormin' critter," Samantha Ann Milliken called him; but if he had held up his head and straightened his broad shoulders, he would have been thought a man of splendid presence.

He seemed a being from another sphere instead of from another section of the country. It was not alone the olive tint of the skin, the mass of wavy dark hair tossed back from a high forehead, the sombre eyes, and the sad mouth,—a mouth that had never grown into laughing curves through telling Yankee jokes,—it was not these that gave him what the boys called a "kind of a downcasted look." The man from Tennessee had something more than a melancholy temperament; he had, or physiognomy was a lie, a sorrow tugging at his heart.

"I'm goin' to doze a spell," drawled Jabe Slocum, pulling his straw hat over his eyes. "I've got to renew my strength like the eagle's, 'f I'm goin' to walk to the circus this afternoon. Wake me up, boys, when you think I'd ought to sling that scythe some more, for if I hev it on my mind I can't git a wink o' sleep."

This was apparently a witticism; at any rate, it elicited roars of laughter.

"It's one of Jabe's useless days; he takes 'em from his great-aunt Lyddy," said David Milliken.

"You jest dry up, Dave. Ef it took me as long to git to workin' as it did you to git a wife, I bate this hay wouldn't git mowed down to crack o' doom. Gorry! ain't this a tree! I tell you, the sun 'n' the airth, the dew 'n' the showers, 'n' the Lord God o' creation jest took holt 'n' worked together on this tree, 'n' no mistake!"

"You're right, Jabe." (This from Steve Webster, who was absently cutting a *D* in the bark. He was always cutting *D*'s these days.) "This ellum can't be beat in the State o' Maine, nor no other state. My brother that lives in California says that the big redwoods, big as they air, don't throw no sech shade, nor ain't so han'some, 'specially in the fall o' the year, as our State o' Maine trees; 'assiduous trees,' he called 'em."

"*Assidyus* trees? Why don't you talk United States while you're about it, 'n' not fire yer long-range words round here? *Assidyus!* What does it mean, anyhow?"

"Can't prove it by me. That's what he called 'em, 'n' I never forgot it."

"Assidyus—assidyus—it don't sound as if it meant nothing', to me."

"Assiduous means 'busy,'" said the man from Tennessee, who had suddenly waked from a brown study, and dropped off into another as soon as he had given the definition.

"Busy, does it? Wall, I guess we ain't no better off now 'n we ever was. One tree's 'bout 's busy as another, as fur 's I can see."

"Wall, there is kind of a meanin' in it to me, but it'sturrible far fetched," remarked Jabe Slocum, rather sleepily. "You see, our ellums and maples 'n' all them trees spends part o' the year in buddin' 'n' gittin' out their leaves 'n' hangin' em all over the branches; 'n' then, no sooner air they full grown than they hev to begin colorin' of 'em red or yeller or brown, 'n' then shakin' 'em off; 'n' this is all extry, you might say, to their every-day chores o' growin' 'n' cirkerlatin' sap, 'n' spreadin' 'n' thickenin' 'n' shovin' out limbs, 'n' one thing 'n' 'nother; 'n' it stan's to reason that the first 'n' hemlocks 'n' them California redwoods, that keeps their clo'es on right through the year, can't be so busy as them that keeps a-dressin' 'n' ondressin' all the time."

"I guess you're 'bout right," allowed Steve, "but I shouldn't never 'a' thought of it in the world. What yer takin' out o' that bottle, Jabe? I thought you was a temperance man."

"I guess he 's like the feller over to Shandagee schoolhouse, that said he was in favor o' the law, but agin its enforcement!" laughed Pitt Packard.

"I ain't breakin' no law; this is yarb bitters," Jabe answered, with a pull at the bottle.

"It's to cirkerlate his blood," said Ob Tarbox; "he's too dog-goned lazy to cirkerlate it himself."

"I'm takin' it fer what ails me," said Jabe oracularly; "the heart knoweth its own bitterness, 'n' it 's a wise child that knows its own complaints 'thout goin' to a doctor."

"Ain't yer scared fer fear it'll start yer growth, Laigs?" asked little Brad Gibson, looking at Jabe's tremendous length of limb and foot. "Say, how do yer git them feet o' yourn uphill? Do yer start one ahead, 'n' side-track the other?"

The tree rang with the laughter evoked by this sally, but the man from Tennessee never smiled.

Jabe Slocum's imperturbable good humor was not shaken in the very least by these personal remarks. "If I thought 't was a good growin' medicine, I'd recommend it to your folks, Brad," he replied cheerfully. "Your mother says you boys air all so short that when you're diggin' potatoes, yer can't see her shake the dinner rag 'thout gittin' up 'n' standing on the potato hills! If I was a sinikitin feller like you, I wouldn't hector folks that had made out to grow some."

"Speakin' o' growin'," said Steve Webster, "who do you guess I seen in Boston, when I was workin' there? That tall Swatkins girl from the Duck Pond, the one that married Dan Robinson. It was one Sunday, in the Catholic meetin'-house. I'd allers wanted to go to a Catholic meetin', an' I declare it's about the solemnest one there is. I mistrusted I was goin' to everlastin'ly giggle, but I tell yer I was the awedest cutter yer ever see. But anyway, the Swatkins girl—or Mis' Robinson, she is now—was there as large as life in the next pew to me, jabberin' Latin, pawin' beads, gettin' up 'n' kneelin' down, 'n' crossin' herself north, south, east, 'n' west, with the best of 'em. Poor Dan! 'Grinnin' Dan,' we used to call him. Well, he don't grin nowadays. He never was good for much, but he 's hed more 'n his comeuppance!"

"Why, what 's the matter with him? Can't he git work in Boston?"

"Matter? Why, his wife, that I see makin' believe be so dreadful pious in the Catholic meetin', she 's carried on wuss 'n the Old Driver for two years, 'n' now she 's up 'n' left him,—gone with a han'somer man."

Down on Steve Webster's hand came Jabe Slocum's immense paw with a grasp that made him cringe.

"What the"—began Steve, when the man from Tennessee took up his scythe and slouched away from the group by the tree.

"Didn't yer know no better 'n that, yer thunderin' fool? Can't yer see a hole in a grindstun 'thout it's hung on yer nose?"

"What hev I done?" asked Steve, as if dumfounded.

"Done? Where 've yer ben, that yer don't know Dixie's wife 's left him?"

"Where 've I ben? Hain't I ben workin' in Boston fer a year; 'n' since I come home last week, hain't I ben tendin' sick folks, so 't I couldn't git outside the dooryard? I never seen the man in my life till yesterday, in the field, 'n' I thought he was one o' them dark-skinned Frenchies from Guildford that hed come up here fer hayin'."

"Mebbe I spoke too sharp," said Jabe apologetically; "but we 've ben scared to talk wives, or even women folks, fer a month o' Sundays, fer fear Dixie 'd up 'n' tumble on his scythe, or do somethin' crazy. You see it's this way (I'd ruther talk than work; 'n' we ain't workin' by time to-day, anyway, on account of the circus comin'): 'Bout a year 'n' a half ago, this tall, han'some feller turned up here in Pleasant River. He inhailed from down South somewheres, but he didn't like his work there, 'n' drifted to New York, 'n' then to Boston; 'n' then he remembered his mother was a State o' Maine woman, 'n' he come here to see how he liked. We didn't take no stock in him at first,—we never hed one o' that nigger-tradin' secedin' lot in amongst us,—but he was pleasant spoken 'n' a square, all-round feller, 'n' didn't git off any secesh nonsense, 'n' it ended in our likin' him first-rate. Wall, he got work in the cannin' fact'ry over on the Butterfield road, 'n' then he fell in with the Maddoxes. You 've hearn tell of 'em; they're relation to Pitt here."

"I wouldn't own 'em if I met 'em on Judgement Bench!" exclaimed Pitt Packard hotly. "My stepfather's second wife married Mis' Maddox's first husband after he got divorced from her, 'n' that's all there is to it; they ain't no bloody-kin o' mine, 'n' I don't call 'em relation."

"Wall, Pitt's relations or not, they're all wuss 'n the Old Driver, as yer said 'bout Dan Robinson's wife. Dixie went to board there. Mis Maddox was all out o' husbands jest then,—she 'd jest disposed of her fourth, somehow or 'nother; she always hed a plenty 'n' to spare, though there's lots o' likely women folks round here that never hed one chance, let alone four. Her daughter Fidelity was a chip o' the old block. Her father hed named her Fidelity after his mother, when she wa'n't nothin' but a two-days-old baby, 'n' he didn't know how she was goin' to turn out; if he 'd 'a' waited two months, I believe I could 'a' told him. *In*fidelity would 'a' ben a mighty sight more 'propriate; but either of 'em is too long fer a name, so they got to callin' her Fiddy. Wall, Fiddy didn't waste no time; she was nigh onto eighteen years old when Dixie went there to board, 'n' she begun huneyfuglin' him's soon as ever she set eyes on him. Folks warned him, but 't wa'n't no use; he was kind o' bewitched with her from the first. She wa'n't so han'some, neither. Blamed 'f I know how they do it; let 'em alone, 'f yer know when yer 're well off, 's my motter. She was red-headed, but her hair become her somehow when she curled 'n' frizzed it over a karosene lamp, 'n' then wound it round 'n' round her head like ropes o' carnelian. She hedn't any particular kind of a nose nor mouth nor eyes, but gorry! when she looked at yer, yer felt kind as if yer was turnin' to putty inside."

"I know what yer mean," said Steve interestedly.

"She hed a figger jest like them fashion-paper pictures you 've seen, an' the very day any new styles come to Boston Fiddy Maddox would hev 'em before sundown; the biggest bustles 'n' the highest hats 'n' the tightest skirts 'n' the longest tails to 'em; she'd git 'em somehow, anyhow! Dixie wa'n't out o' money when he come here, an' a spell afterwards there was more 'n a thousand dollars fell to him from his father's folks down South. Well, Fiddy made that fly, I tell you! Dixie bought a top buggy 'n' a sorrel hoss, 'n' they was on the road most o' the time when he wa'n't to work; 'n' when he was, she 'd go with Lem Simmons, 'n' Dixie none the wiser. Mis Maddox was lookin' up a new husband jest then, so 't she didn't interfere"—

"She was the same kind o' goods, anyhow," interpolated Ob Tarbox.

"Yes, she was one of them women folks that air so light-minded you can't anchor 'em down with a sewin'-machine, nor a dishpan, nor a husband 'n' young ones, nor no namable kind of a thing; the least wind blows 'em here 'n' blows 'em there, like dandelion puffs. As time went on, the widder got herself a beau now 'n' then; but as fast as she hooked 'em, Fiddy up 'n' took 'em away from her. You see she 'd gethered in most of her husbands afore Fiddy was old enough to hev her finger in the pie; but she cut her eye-teeth early, Fiddy did, 'n' there wa'n't no kind of a feller come to set up with the widder but she 'd everlastin'ly grab him, if she hed any use fer him, 'n' then there 'd be Hail Columby, I tell yer. But Dixie, he was 's blind 's a bat 'n' deef 's a post. He could n't see nothin' but Fiddy, 'n' he couldn't see her very plain."

"He hed warnin's enough," put in Pitt Packard, though Jabe Slocum never needed any assistance in spinning a yarn.

"Warnin's! I should think he hed. The Seventh Day Baptist minister went so fur as to preach at him. 'The Apostle Paul gin heed,' was the text. 'Why did he gin heed?' says he. 'Because he heerd. If he hadn't 'a' heerd, he couldn't 'a' gin heed, 'n' 't wouldn't 'a' done him no good to 'a' heerd 'thout he gin heed!' Wall, it helped consid'ble many in the congregation, 'specially them that was in the habit of hearin' 'n' heedin', but it rolled right off Dixie like water off a duck's back. He 'n' Fiddy was seen over to the ballin' alley to Wareham next day, 'n' they didn't come back for a week."

"He gin her his hand,

And he made her his own,'"

sang little Brad Gibson.

"He hed gin her his hand, but no minister nor trial-jestice nor eighteen-carat ring nor stificate could 'a' made Fiddy Maddox anybody's own 'ceptin' the devil's, an' he wouldn't 'a' married her; she'd 'a' ben too near kin. We'd never 'spicioned she 'd git 's fur 's marryin' anybody, 'n' she only married Dixie 'cause he told her he 'd take her to the Wareham House to dinner, 'n' to the County Fair afterwards; if any other feller hed offered to take her to supper, 'n' the theatre on top o' that, she 'd 'a' married him instid."

"How 'd the old woman take it?" asked Steve.

"She disowned her daughter *punctilio:* in the first place, fer runnin' away 'stid o' hevin' a church weddin'; 'n' second place, fer marryin' a pauper (that was what she called him; 'n' it was true, for they 'd spent every cent he hed); 'n' third place, fer alienatin' the 'fections of a travelin' baker-man she hed her eye on fer herself. He was a kind of a flour-food peddler, that used to drive a cart round by Hard Scrabble, Moderation, 'n' Scratch Corner way. Mis' Maddox used to buy all her baked victuals of him, 'specially after she found out he was a widower beginnin' to take notice. His cart used to stand at her door so long everybody on the rout would complain o' stale bread. But bime bye Fiddy begun to set at her winder when he druv up, 'n' bime bye she pinned a blue ribbon in her collar. When she done that, Mis' Maddox alles hed to take a back seat. The boys used to call it a danger signal. It kind o' drawed yer 'tention to p'ints 'bout her chin 'n' mouth 'n' neck, 'n' one thing 'n' 'nother, in a way that was cal'lated to snarl up the thoughts o' perfessors o' religion 'n' turn 'em earthways. There was a spell I hed to say, *'Remember Rhapseny! Remember Rhapseny!* over to myself whenever Fiddy put on her blue ribbons. Wall, as I say, Fiddy set at the winder, the baker-man seen the blue ribbons, 'n' Mis' Maddox's cake was dough. She put on a red ribbon; but land! her neck looked 's if somebody 'd gone over it with a harrer! Then she stomped round 'n' slat the dish-rag, but 't wa'n't no use. 'Gracious, mother,' says Fiddy, 'I don't do nothin' but set at the winder. The sun shines for all.' 'You're right it does,' says Mis' Maddox, "n' that's jest what I complain of. I'd like to get a change to shine on something myself.'

"But the baker-man kep' on comin', though when he got to the Maddoxes' doorsteps he couldn't make change for a quarter nor tell pie from bread; an' sure 's you're born, the very day Fiddy went away to be married to Dixie, that mornin' she drawed that everlastin' numhead of a flour-food peddler out into the orchard, 'n' cut off a lock o' her hair, 'n' tied it up with a piece o' her blue ribbon, 'n' give it to him; an' old Mis' Bascom says, when he went past her house he was gazin' at it 'n' kissin' of it, 'n' his horse meanderin' on one side the road 'n' the other, 'n' the door o' the cart open 'n' slammin' to 'n' fro, 'n' ginger cookies spillin' out all over the lot. He come back to the Maddoxes next mornin' ('t wa'n't his day, but his hoss couldn't pull one way when Fiddy's ribbon was pullin' t'other); an' when he found out she 'd gone with Dixie, he cussed 'n' stomped 'n' took on like a loontic; an' when Mis' Maddox hinted she was ready to heal the wownds Fiddy 'd inflicted, he stomped 'n' cussed wuss 'n' ever, 'n' the neighbors say he called her a hombly old trollop, an' fired the bread loaves all over the dooryard, he was so crazy at bein' cheated.

"Wall, to go back to Dixie—I'll be comin' right along, boys." (This to Brad Gibson, who was taking his farewell drink of ginger tea preparatory to beginning work.)

"I pity you, Steve!" exclaimed Brad, between deep swallows. "If you 'd known when you was well off, you 'd 'a' stayed in Boston. If Jabe hed a story started, he 'd talk three days after he was dead."

"Go 'long; leave me be! Wall, as I was sayin', Dixie brought Fiddy home ('Dell,' he called her), an' they 'peared bride 'n' groom at meetin' next Sunday. The last hundred dollars he hed in the world hed gone into the weddin' tower 'n' on to Fiddy's back. He hed a new suit, 'n' he looked like a major. You ain't got no idea what he was, 'cause his eyes is dull now, 'n' he 's bowed all over, 'n' ain't shaved nor combed, hardly; but they was the han'somest couple that ever walked up the broad aisle. She hed on a green silk dress, an' a lace cape that was like a skeeter nettin' over her neck an' showed her bare skin through, an' a hat like an apple orchard in full bloom, hummin'-bird an' all. Dixie kerried himself as proud as Lucifer. He didn't look at the minister 'n' he didn't look at the congregation; his great eyes was glued on Fiddy, as if he couldn't hardly keep from eatin' of her up. An' she behaved consid'able well for a few months, as long 's the novelty lasted an' the silk dresses was new. Before Christmas, though, she began to peter out 'n' git slack-twisted. She allers hated housework as bad as a pig would a penwiper, an' Dixie hed to git his own breakfast afore he went to work, or go off on an empty stomach. Many 's the time he 's got her meals for her 'n' took 'em to her on a waiter. Them secesh fellers'll wait on women folks long as they can stan' up.

"Then bime bye the baby come along; but that made things wuss 'stid o' better. She didn't pay no more 'tention to it than if it hed belonged to the town. She 'd go off to dances, an' leave Dixie to home tendin' cradle; but that wa'n't no hardship to him for he was 'bout as much wropped up in the child as he was in Fiddy. Wall, sir, 'bout a month ago she up 'n' disappeared off the face o' the airth 'thout sayin' a word or leavin' a letter. She took her clo'es, but she never thought o' takin' the baby; one baby more or less didn't make no odds to her s' long 's she hed that skeeter-nettin' cape. Dixie sarched fer her high an' low fer a fortnight, but after that he give it up as a bad job. He found out enough, I guess, to keep him pretty busy thinkin' what he 'd do next. But day before yesterday the same circus that plays here this afternoon was playin' to Wareham. A lot of us went over on the evenin' train, an' we coaxed Dixie into goin', so 's to take his mind off his trouble. But land! he didn't see nothin'. He 'd walk right up the lions 'n' tigers in the menagerie as if they was cats 'n' chickens, an' all the time the clown was singin' he looked like a dumb animile that 's hed a bullet put in him. There was lots o' side shows, mermaids 'n' six-legged calves 'n' spotted girls, 'n' one thing 'n' 'nother, an' there was one o' them whirligig machines with a mess o' rocking'-hosses goin' round 'n' round, 'n' an organ in the middle playin' like sixty. I wish we 'd 'a' kept clear o' the thing, but as bad luck would hev it, we stopped to look, an' there on top o' two high-steppin' white wooden hosses, set Mis' Fiddy an' that dod-gasted light-complected baker-man! If ever she was suited to a dot, it was jest then 'n' there. She could 'a' gone prancin' round that there ring forever 'n' forever, with the whoopin' 'n' hollerin' 'n' whizzin' 'n' whirlin' soundin' in her ears, 'n' the music playin' like mad, 'n' she with nothin' to do but stick on 'n' let some feller foot the bills. Somebody must 'a' ben thinkin' o' Fiddy Maddox when the invented them whirl-a-go-rounds. She was laughin' 'n' carryin' on like the old Scratch; her apple-blossom hat dome off, 'n' the baker-man put it on, 'n' took consid'able time over it, 'n' pulled her ear 'n' pinched her cheek when he got through; an' that was jest the blamed minute we ketched sight of 'em. I pulled Dixie off, but I was too late. He give a groan I shall remember to my dyin' day, 'n' then he plunged out o' the crowd 'n' through the gate like a streak o' lightnin'. We follered, but land! we couldn't find him, an' true as I set here, I never expected to see him alive agin. But I did; I forgot all about one thing, you see, 'n' that was the baby. If it wa'n't no attraction to its mother, I guess he cal'lated it needed a father all the more. Anyhow, he turned up in the field yesterday mornin', ready for work, but lookin' as if he 'd hed his heart cut out 'n' a piece o' lead put in the place of it."

"I don't seem as if she 'd 'a' ben brazen enough to come back so near him," said Steve.

"Wall, I don't s'pose she hed any idea o' Dixie's bein' at a circus over Wareham jest then; an' ten to one she didn't care if the whole town seen her. She wanted to get rid of him, 'n' she didn't mind how she did it. Dixie ain't one of the shootin' kinds, an' anyhow, Fiddy Maddox wa'n't one to look ahead; whatever she wanted to do, that she done, from the time she was knee high to a grasshopper. I've seen her set down by a peck basket of apples, 'n' take a couple o' bites out o' one, 'n' then heave it fur 's she could heave it 'n' start in on another, 'n' then another; 'n' 't wa'n't a good apple year, neither. She'd everlastin'ly spile 'bout a dozen of 'em 'n' smaller 'bout two mouthfuls. Doxy Morton, now, would eat an apple clean down to the core, 'n' then count the seeds 'n' put 'em on the window-sill to dry, 'n' get up 'n' put the core in the stove, 'n' wipe her hands on the roller towel, 'n' take up her sewin' agin; 'n' if you 've got to be cuttin' 'nitials in tree bark an' writin' of 'em in the grass with a stick like you 've ben doin' for the last half-hour, you 're blamed lucky to be doin' *D*'s not *F*'s, like Dixie there!"

It was three o'clock in the afternoon. The men had dropped work and gone to the circus. The hay was pronounced to be in a condition where it could be left without much danger; but, for that matter, no man would have stayed in the field to attend to another man's hay when there was a circus in the neighborhood.

Dixie was mowing on alone, listening as in a dream to that subtle something in the swish of the scythe that makes one seek to know the song it is singing to the grasses.

> *"Hush, ah, hush, the scythes are saying,*
>
> *Hush, and heed not, and fall asleep;*
>
> *Hush, they say to the grasses swaying,*
>
> *Hush, they sing to the clover deep;*
>
> *Hush,—'t is the lullaby Time is singing,—*
>
> *Hush, and heed not, for all things pass.*
>
> *Hush, ah, hush! and the scythes are swinging*
>
> *Over the clover, over the grass."*

And now, spent with fatigue and watching and care and grief,—heart sick, mind sick, body sick, sick with past suspense and present certainty and future dread,—he sat under the cool shade of the nooning tree, and buried his face in his hands. He was glad to be left alone with his miseries,—glad that the other men, friendly as he felt them to be, had gone to the circus, where he would not see or hear them for hours to come.

How clearly he could conjure up the scene that they were enjoying with such keen relish! Only two days before, he had walked among the same tents, staring at horses and gay trappings and painted Amazons as one who noted nothing; yet the agony of the thing he now saw at last lit up all the rest as with a lightning flash, and burned the scene forever on his brain and heart. It was at Wareham, too,—Wareham, where she had promised to be his wife, where she had married him only a year before. How well he remembered the night! They left the parsonage; they had ten miles to drive in the moonlight before reaching their stopping-place,—ten miles of such joy as only a man could know, he thought, who had had the warm fruit of life hanging within full vision, but just out of reach,—just above his longing lips; and then, in an unlooked-for, gracious moment, his! He could swear she had loved him that night, if never again.

But this picture passed away, and he saw that maddening circle with the caracoling steeds. He head the discordant music, the monotonous creak of the machinery, the strident laughter of the excited riders. As first the thing was a blur, a kaleidoscope of whirling colors, into which there presently crept form and order. ... A boy who had cried to get on, and was now crying to get off. ... Old Rube Hobson and his young wife; Rube looking white and scared, partly by the whizzing motion, and partly by the prospect of paying out ten cents for the doubtful pleasure. ... Pretty Hetty Dunnell with that young fellow from Portland; she too timid to mount one of the mettle-some chargers, and snuggling close to him in one of the circling seats. The, good Got!—Dell! sitting on a prancing white horse, with the man he knew, the man he feared, riding beside her; a man who kept holding on her hat with fingers that trembled,—the very hat she "'peared bride in" a man who brushed a grasshopper from her shoulder with an air of ownership, and, when she slapped his hand coquettishly, even dared to pinch her pink cheek,—his wife's cheek,—before that crowd of on-lookers! Merry-go-round, indeed! The horrible thing was well named; and life was just like it,—a whirl of happiness and misery, in which the music cannot play loud enough to drown the creak of the machinery, in which one soul cries out in pain, another in terror, and the rest laugh; but the prancing steeds gallop on, gallop on, and once mounted, there is no getting off, unless...

There were some things it was not possible for a mean to bear! The river! The river! He could hear it rippling over the sunny sands, swirling among the logs, dashing and roaring under the bridge, rushing to the sea's embrace. Could it tell whither it was hurrying? NO; but it was escaping from its present bonds; it would never have to pass over these same jagged rocks again. "On, on to the unknown!" called the river. "I come! I come!" he roused himself to respond, when a faint, faint, helpless voice broke in upon the mad clatter in his brain, cleaving his torn heart in twain; not a real voice,—the half-forgotten memory of one; a tender wail that had added fresh misery to his night's vigil,—the baby!

But the feeble pipe was borne down by the swirl of the water as it dashed between the rocky banks, still calling to him. If he could only close his ears to it! But it still called—called still—the river! And still the child's voice pierced the rush of sound with its pitiful flute note, until the two resolved themselves into contesting strains, answering each other antiphonally. The river—the baby—the river—the baby; and in and through, and betwixt and between, there spun the whirling merry-go-round, with its curveting wooden horses, its discordant organ, and its creaking machinery.

But gradually the child's voice gained in strength, and as he heard it more plainly the other sounds grew fainter, till at last, thank God! they were hushed. The din, the whirlwind, and the tempest in his brain were lulled into silence, as under a "Peace, be still!" and, worn out with the contest, the man from Tennessee fell asleep under the grateful shade of the nooning tree. So deep was the slumber that settled over exhausted body and troubled spirit that the gathering clouds, the sudden darkness, the distant muttering of thunder, the frightened twitter of the birds, passed unnoticed. A heavy drop of rain pierced the thick foliage and fell on his face, but the storm within had been too fierce for him to heed the storm without. He slept on.

Almost every man, woman, and child in the vicinity of Pleasant River was on the way to the circus,—Boomer's Grand Six-in-One Universal Consolidated Show; Brilliant Constellations of Fixed Stars shining in the same Vast Firmament; Glittering Galaxies of World-Famous Equestrian Artists; the biggest elephants, the funniest clowns, the pluckiest riders, the stubbornest mules, the most amazing acrobats, the tallest man and the shortest man, the thinnest woman and the thickest woman, on the habitable globe; and no connection with any other show on earth, especially Sypher's Two-in-One Show now devastating the same State.

If the advertisements setting forth these attractions were couched in language somewhat rosier than the facts would warrant, there were few persons calm enough to perceive it, when once the glamour of the village parade and the smell of the menagerie had intoxicated the senses.

The circus had been the sole topic of conversation for a fortnight. Jot Bascom could always be relied on for the latest and most authentic news of its triumphant progress from one town to another. Jot was a sort of town crier; and whenever the approach of a caravan was announced, he would go over on the Liberty road to find out just where it was and what were its immediate plans, for the thrilling pleasure of calling at every one of the neighbors' on his way home, and delivering his budget of news. He was an attendant at every funeral, and as far as possible at every wedding, in the village; at every flag-raising and husking, and town and county fair. When more pressing duties did not hinder, he endeavored to meet the two daily trains that passed through Milliken's Mills, a mile or two from Pleasant River. He accompanied the sheriff on all journeys entailing serving of papers and other embarrassing duties common to the law. On one occasion, when the two lawyers of the village held an investigation before Trial Justice Simeon Porter, they waited an hour because Jot Bascom did not come. They knew that something was amiss, but it was only on reflection that they remembered that Jot was not indispensable. He went with all paupers to the Poor Farm, and never missed a town meeting. He knew all the conditions attending any swapping of horses that occurred within a radius of twenty miles,—the terms of the trade and the amount paid to boot. He knew who owed the fish-man and who owed the meat-man, and who could not get trusted by either of them. In fact, so far as the divine attributes of omniscience and omnipresence could be vested in a faulty human creature, they were present in Jot Bascom. That he was quite unable to attend conscientiously to home duties, when overborne by press of public service, was true. When Diadema Bascom wanted kindling split, wood brought in, the cows milked, or the pigs fed, she commonly found her spouse serving humanity in bulk.

All the details of the approach of the Grand Six-in-One Show had, therefore, been heralded to those work-sodden and unambitious persons who tied themselves to their own wood-piles or haying-fields.

These were the bulletins issues:—

The men were making a circle in the Widow Buzzell's field, in the same place where the old one had been,—the old one, viewed with awe for five years by all the village small boys.

The forerunners, outriders, proprietors, whatever they might be, had arrived and gone to the tavern.

An elephant was quartered in the tavern shed!

The elephant had stepped through the floor!!

The advance guard of performers and part of the show itself had come!

And the "Cheriot"!!

This far-famed vehicle had paused on top of Deacon Chute's hill, to prepare for the street parade. Little Jim Chute had been gloating over the fact that it must pass by his house, and when it stopped short under the elms in the dooryard his heart almost broke for joy. He pinched the twenty-five-cent piece in his pocket to assure himself that he was alive and in his right mind.

The precious coin had been the result of careful saving, and his hot, excited hands had almost worn it thin. But alas for the vanity of human hopes! When the magnificent red-and-gold "Cheriot" was uncovered, that its glories might shine upon the waiting world, the door opened, and a huddle of painted Indians tumbled out, ready to lead the procession, or, if so disposed, to scalp the neighborhood. Little Jim gave one panic-stricken look as they leaped over the chariot steps, and then fled to the barn chamber, whence he had to be dragged by his mother, and cuffed into willingness to attend the spectacle that had once so dazzled his imagination.

On the eventful afternoon of the performance the road was gay with teams. David and Samantha Milliken drove by in Miss Cummin's neat carryall, two children on the back seat, a will-o'-the-wisp baby girl held down by a serious boy. Steve Webster was driving Doxy Morton in his mother's buggy. Jabe Slocum, Pitt Packard, Brad Gibson, Cyse Higgins, and scores of others were riding "shank's mare," as they would have said.

It had been a close, warm day, and as the afternoon wore away it grew hotter and closer. There was a dead calm in the air, a threatening blackness in the west that made the farmers think anxiously of their hay. Presently the thunderheads ran together into big black clouds, which melted in turn into molten masses of smoky orange, so that the heavens were like burnished brass. Drivers whipped up their horses, and pedestrians hastened their steps. Steve Webster decided not to run even the smallest risk of injuring so precious a commodity as Doxy Morton by a shower of rain, so he drove into a friend's yard, put up his horse, and waited till the storm should pass by. Brad Gibson stooped to drink at a wayside brook, and as he bent over the water he heard a low, murmuring, muttering sound that seemed to make the earth tremble.

Then from hill to hill "leapt the live thunder." Even the distant mountains seemed to have "found a tongue." A zigzag chain of lightning flashed in the lurid sky, and after an appreciable interval another peal, louder than the first, and nearer.

The rain began to fall, the forked flashes of flame darted hither and thither in the clouds, and the boom of heaven's artillery grew heavier and heavier. The blinding sheets of light and the tumultuous roar of sound now followed each other so quickly that they seemed almost simultaneous. Flash—crash—flash—crash—flash—crash; blinding and deafening eye and ear at once. Everybody who could find a shelter of any sort hastened to it. The women at home set their children in the midst of feather beds, and some of them even huddled there themselves, their babies clinging to them in sympathetic fear, as the livid shafts of light illuminated the dark rooms with more than noonday glare.

The air was full of gloom; a nameless terror lurked within it; the elements seemed at war with each other. Horses whinnied in the stables, and colts dashed about the pastures. The cattle sought sheltered places; the cows ambling clumsily towards some refuge, their full bags dripping milk as they swung heavily to and fro. The birds flew towards the orchards and the deep woods; the swallows swooped restlessly round the barns, and hid themselves under the eaves or in the shadow of deserted nests.

The rain now fell in sheets.

"Hurry up 'n' git under cover, Jabe," said Brad Gibson; "you're jest the kind of a pole to draw lightnin'!"

"You hain't, then!" retorted Jabe. "There ain't enough o' you fer lightnin' to ketch holt of!"

Suddenly a ghastly streak of light leaped out of a cloud, and then another, till the sky seemed lit up by cataracts of flame. A breath of wind sprang into the still air. Then a deafening crash, clap, crack, roar, peal! and as Jabe Slocum looked out of a protecting shed door, he saw a fiery ball burst from the clouds, shooting brazen arrows as it fell. Within the instant the meeting-house steeple broke into a tongue of flame, and then, looking towards home, he fancied that the fireball dropped to earth in Squire Bean's meadow.

The wind blew more fiercely now. There was a sudden crackling of wood, falling of old timers, and breaking of glass. The deadly fluid ran in a winding course down a great maple by the shed, leaving a narrow charred channel through the bark to tell how it passed to earth. A sombre pine stood up, black and burned, its heart gaping through a ghastly wound in the split trunk.

The rain now subsided; there was only an occasional faint rumbling of thunder, as if it were murmuring over the distant sea; the clouds broke away in the west; the sun peeped out, as if to see what had been going on in the world since he hid himself an hour before. A delicate rainbow bridge stretched from the blackened church steeple to the glittering weathercock on the squire's barn; and there, in the centre of the fair green meadows from which it had risen in glorious strength and beauty for a century or more, lay the nooning tree.

The fireball, if ball of fire indeed there were, had struck in the very centre of its splendid dome, and ploughed its way from feather tip to sturdy root, riving the tree in twain, cleaving its great boughs left and right, laying one majestic half level with the earth, and bending the other till the proud head almost touched the grass.

The rainbow was reflected in the million drops glittering upon the bowed branches, turning each into a tear of liquid opal. The birds hopped on the prone magnificence, and eyed timorously a strange object underneath.

There had been one swift, pitiless, merciful stroke! The monarch of the meadow would never again feel the magic thrill of the sap in its veins, nor the bursting of brown bud into green leaf.

The birds would build their nests and sing their idyls in other boughs. The "time of pleasure and love" was over with the nooning tree; over too, with him who slept beneath; for under its fallen branches, with the light of a great peace in his upturned face, lay the man from Tennessee.

THE FORE-ROOM RUG.

Diadema, wife of Jot Bascom, was sitting at the window of the village watch-tower, so called because it commanded a view of nearly everything that happened in Pleasant River; those details escaping the physical eye being supplied by faith and imagination working in the light of past experience. She sat in the chair of honor, the chair of choice, the high-backed rocker by the southern window, in which her husband's mother, old Mrs. Bascom, had sat for thirty years, applying a still more powerful intellectual telescope to the doings of her neighbors. Diadema's seat had formerly been on the less desirable side of the little light-stand, where Priscilla Hollis was now installed.

Mrs. Bascom was at work on a new fore-room rug, the former one having been transferred to Miss Hollis's chamber; for, as the teacher at the brick schoolhouse, a graduate of a Massachusetts normal school, and the daughter of a deceased judge, she was a boarder of considerable consequence. It was a rainy Saturday afternoon, and the two women were alone. It was a pleasant, peaceful sitting-room, as neat as wax in every part. The floor was covered by a cheerful patriotic rag carpet woven entirely of red, white, and blue rags, and protected in various exposed localities by button rugs,—red, white, and blue disks superimposed one on the other.

Diadema Bascom was a person of some sentiment. When her old father, Captain Dennett, was dying, he drew a wallet from under his pillow, and handed her a twenty-dollar bill to get something to remember him by. This unwonted occurrence burned itself into the daughter's imagination, and when she came as a bride to the Bascom house she refurnished the sitting-room as a kind of monument to the departed soldier, whose sword and musket were now tied to the wall with neatly hemmed bows of bright red cotton.

The chair cushions were of red-and-white glazed patch, the turkey wings that served as hearth brushes were hung against the white-painted chimney-piece with blue skirt braid, and the white shades were finished with home-made scarlet "tossels." A little whatnot in one corner was laden with the trophies of battle. The warrior's brass buttons were strung on a red picture cord and hung over his daguerreotype on the upper shelf; there was a tarnished shoulder strap, and a flattened bullet that the captain's jealous contemporaries swore *he* never stopped, unless he got it in the rear when he was flying from the foe. There was also a little tin canister in which a charge of powder had been sacredly preserved. The scoffers, again, said that "the cap'n put it in his musket when he went into the war, and kep' it there till he come out." These objects were tastefully decorated with the national colors. In fact, no modern aesthete could have arranged a symbolic symphony of grief and glory with any more fidelity to an ideal than Diadema Bascom, in working out her scheme of red, white, and blue.

Rows of ripening tomatoes lay along the ledges of the windows, and a tortoise-shell cat snoozed on one of the broad sills. The tall clock in the corner ticked peacefully. Priscilla Hollis never tired of looking at the jolly red-cheeked moon, the group of stars on a blue ground, the trig little ship, the old house, and the jolly moon again, creeping one after another across the open space at the top.

Jot Bascom was out, as usual, gathering statistics of the last horse trade; little Jot was building "stickin'" houses in the barn; Priscilla was sewing long strips for braiding; while Diadema sat at the drawing-in frame, hook in hand, and a large basket of cut rags by her side.

Not many weeks before she had paid one of her periodical visits to the attic. No housekeeper in Pleasant River save Mrs. Jonathan Bascom would have thought of dusting a garret, washing the window and sweeping down the cobwebs once a month, and renewing the camphor bags in the chests twice a year; but notwithstanding this zealous care the moths had made their way into one of her treasure-houses, the most precious of all,—the old hair trunk that had belonged to her sister Lovice. Once ensconced there, they had eaten through its hoarded relics, and reduced the faded finery to a state best described by Diadema as "reg'lar riddlin' sieves." She had brought the tattered pile down in to the kitchen, and had spent a tearful afternoon in cutting the good pieces from the perforated garments. Three heaped-up baskets and a full dish-pan were the result; and as she had snipped and cut and sorted, one of her sentimental projects had entered her mind and taken complete possession there.

"I declare," she said, as she drew her hooking-needle in and out, "I wouldn't set in the room with some folks and work on these pieces; for every time I draw in a scrap of cloth Lovice comes up to me for all the world as if she was settin' on the sofy there. I ain't told you my plan, Miss Hollis, and there ain't many I shall tell; but this rug is going to be a kind of a hist'ry of my life and Lovey's wrought in together, just as we was bound up in one another when she was alive. Her things and mine was laid in one trunk, and the moths sha'n't cheat me out of 'em altogether. If I can't look at 'em wet Sundays, and shake 'em out, and have a good cry over 'em, I'll make 'em up into a kind of dumb show that will mean something to me, if it don't to anybody else.

"We was the youngest of thirteen, Lovey and I, and we was twins. There's never been more 'n half o' me left sence she died. We was born together, played and went to school together, got engaged and married together, and we all but died together, yet we wa'n't a mite alike. There was an old lady come to our house once that used to say, 'There's sister Nabby, now: she 'n'

I ain't no more alike 'n if we wa'n't two; she 's jest as diff'rent as I am t' other way.' Well, I know what I want to put into my rag story, Miss Hollis, but I don't hardly know how to begin."

Priscilla dropped her needle, and bent over the frame with interest.

"A spray of two roses in the centre,—there 's the beginning; why, don't you see, dear Mrs. Bascom?"

"Course I do," said Diadema, diving to the bottom of the dish-pan. "I've got my start now, and don't you say a word for a minute. The two roses grow out of one stalk; they'll be Lovey and me, though I'm consid'able more like a potato blossom. The stalk 's got to be green, and here is the very green silk mother walked bride in, and Lovey and I had roundabouts of it afterwards. She had the chicken-pox when we was about four years old, and one of the first things I can remember is climbing up and looking over mother's footboard at Lovey, all speckled. Mother had let her slip on her new green roundabout over her nightgown, just to pacify her, and there she set playing with the kitten Reuben Granger had brought her. He was only ten years old then, but he 'd begun courting Lovice.

"The Grangers' farm joined ours. They had eleven children, and mother and father had thirteen, and we was always playing together. Mother used to tell a funny story about that. We were all little young ones and looked pretty much alike, so she didn't take much notice of us in the daytime when we was running out 'n' in; but at night when the turn-up bedstead in the kitchen was taken down and the trundle-beds were full, she used to count us over, to see if we were all there. One night, when she 'd counted thirteen and set down to her sewing, father come in and asked if Moses was all right, for one of the neighbors had seen him playing side of the river about supper-time. Mother knew she 'd counted us straight, but she went round with a candle to make sure. Now, Mr. Granger had a head as red as a shumac bush; and when she carried the candle close to the beds to take another tally, there was thirteen children, sure enough, but if there wa'n't a red-headed Granger right in amongst our boys in the turn-up bedstead! While father set out on a hunt for our Moses, mother yanked the sleepy little red-headed Granger out o' the middle and took him home, and father found Moses asleep on a pile of shavings under the joiner's bench.

"They don't have such families nowadays. One time when measles went all over the village, they never came to us, and Jabe Slocum said there wa'n't enough measles to go through the Dennett family, so they didn't start in on 'em. There, I ain't going to finish the stalk; I'm going to draw in a little here and there all over the rug, while I'm in the sperit of plannin' it, and then it will be plain work of matching colors and filling out.

"You see the stalk is mother's dress, and the outside green of the moss roses is the same goods, only it 's our roundabouts. I meant to make 'em red, when I marked the pattern, and then fill out round 'em with a light color; but now I ain't satisfied with anything but white, for nothing will do in the middle of the rug but our white wedding dresses. I shall have to fill in dark, then, or mixed. Well, that won't be out of the way, if it 's going to be a true rag story; for Lovey's life went out altogether, and mine hasn't been any too gay.

"I'll begin on Lovey's rose first. She was the prettiest and the liveliest girl in the village, and she had more beaux than you could shake a stick at. I generally had to take what she left over. Reuben Granger was crazy about her from the time she was knee-high; but when he went away to Bangor to study for the ministry, the others had it all their own way. She was only seventeen; she hadn't ever experienced religion, and she was mischeevous as a kitten.

"You remember you laughed, this morning, when Mr. Bascom told about Hogshead Jowett? Well, he used to want to keep company with Lovey; but she couldn't abide him, and whenever he come to court her she clim' into a hogshead, and hid till after he 'd gone. The boys found it out, and used to call him 'Hogshead Jowett.'" He was the biggest fool in Foxboro' Four Corners; and that 's saying consid'able, for Foxboro' is famous for its fools, and always has been. There was thirteen of 'em there one year. They say a man come out from Portland, and when he got as fur as Foxboro' he kep' inquiring the way to Dunstan; and I declare if he didn't meet them thirteen fools, one after another, standing in their front dooryards ready to answer questions. When he got to Dunstan, says he, 'For the Lord's sake, what kind of a village is that I've just went through? Be they *all* fools there?'

"Hogshead was scairt to death whenever he come to see Lovice. One night, when he 'd been there once, and she 'd hid, as she always done, he come back a second time, and she went to the door, not mistrusting it was him. 'Did you forget anything?' says she, sparkling out at him through a little crack. He was all taken aback by seeing her, and he stammered out, 'Yes, I forgot my han'k'chief; but it don't make no odds, for I didn't pay out but fifteen cents for it two year ago, and I don't make no use of it 'ceptins to wipe my nose on.' How we did laugh over that! Well, he had a conviction of sin pretty soon afterwards, and p'r'aps it helped his head some; at any rate he quit farming, and become a Bullockite preacher.

"It seems odd, when Lovice wa'n't a perfessor herself, she should have drawed the most pious young men in the village, but she did: she had good Orthodox beaux, Free and Close Baptists, Millerites and Adventists, all on her string together; she even had one Cochranite, though the sect had mostly died out. But when Reuben Granger come home, a full-feathered-out minister, he seemed to strike her fancy as he never had before, though they were always good friends from children. He had light hair and blue eyes and fair skin (his business being under cover kep' him bleached out), and he and Lovey made the prettiest couple you ever see; for she was dark complected, and her cheeks no otherways than scarlit the whole durin' time. She had a change of heart that winter; in fact she had two of 'em, for she changed hers for Reuben's, and found a hope at the same time. 'T was a good honest conversion, too, though she did say to me she was afraid that if Reuben hadn't taught her what love was or might be, she 'd never have found out enough about it to love God as she 'd ought to.

"There, I've begun both roses, and hers is 'bout finished. I sha'n't have more 'n enough white alapaca. It's lucky the moths spared one breadth of the wedding dresses; we was married on the same day, you know, and dressed just alike. Jot wa'n't quite ready to be married, for he wa'n't any more forehanded 'bout that than he was 'bout other things; but I told him Lovey and I had kept up with each other from the start, and he 'd got to fall into line or drop out o' the percession.—Now what next?"

"Wasn't there anybody at the wedding but you and Lovice?" asked Priscilla, with an amused smile.

"Land, yes! The meeting-house was cram jam full. Oh, to be sure! I know what you 're driving at! Well, I have to laugh to think I should have forgot the husbands! They'll have to be worked into the story, certain; but it'll be consid'able of a chore, for I can't make flowers out of coat and pants stuff, and there ain't any more flowers on this branch anyway."

Diadema sat for a few minutes in rapt thought, and then made a sudden inspired dash upstairs, where Miss Hollis presently heard her rummaging in an old chest. She soon came down, triumphant.

"Wa'n't it a providence I saved Jot's and Reuben's wedding ties! And here they are,—one yellow and green mixed, and one brown. Do you know what I'm going to do? I'm going to draw in a butterfly hovering over them two roses, and make it out of the neckties,—green with brown spots. That'll bring in the husbands; and land! I wouldn't have either of 'em know it for the world. I'll take a pattern of that lunar moth you pinned on the curtain yesterday."

Miss Hollis smiled in spite of herself. "You have some very ingenious ideas and some very pretty thoughts, Mrs. Bascom, do you know it?"

"It's the first time I ever heard tell of it," said Diadema cheerfully. "Lovey was the pretty-spoken, pretty-appearing one; I was always plain and practical. While I think of it, I'll draw in a little mite of this red into my carnation pink. It was a red scarf Reuben brought Lovey from Portland. It was the first thing he ever give her, and aunt Hitty said if one of the Abel Grangers give away anything that cost money, it meant business. That was all fol-de-rol, for there never was a more liberal husband, though he was a poor minister; but then they always *are* poor, without they're rich; there don't seem to be any halfway in ministers.

"We was both lucky that way. There ain't a stingy bone in Jot Bascom's body. He don't make much money, but what he does make goes into the bureau drawer, and the one that needs it most takes it out. He never asks me what I done with the last five cents he give me. You 've never been married Miss Hollis, and you ain't engaged, so you don't know much about it; but I tell you there 's a heap o' foolishness talked about husbands. If you get the one you like yourself, I don't know as it matters if all the other women folks in town don't happen to like him as well as you do; they ain't called on to do that. They see the face he turns to them, not the one he turns to you. Jot ain't a very good provider, nor he ain't a man that 's much use round a farm, but he 's such a fav'rite I can't blame him. There 's one thing: when he does come home he 's got something to say, and he 's always as lively as a cricket, and smiling as a basket of chips. I like a man that 's good comp'ny, even if he ain't so forehanded. There ain't anything specially lovable about forehandedness, when you come to that. I shouldn't ever feel drawed to a man because he was on time with his work. He 's got such pleasant ways, Jot has! The other afternoon he didn't get home early enough to milk; and after I done the two cows, I split the kindling and brought in the wood, for I knew he 'd want to go to the tavern and tell the boys 'bout the robbery up to Boylston. There ain't anybody but Jot in this village that has wit enough to find out what 's going on, and tell it in an int'resting way round the tavern fire. And he can do it without being full of cider, too; he don't need any apple juice to limber *his* tongue!

"Well, when he come in, he see the pails of milk, and the full wood-box, and the supper laid out under the screen cloth on the kitchen table, and he come up to me at the sink, and says he, 'Diademy, you 're the best wife in this county, and the brightest jewel in my crown,—that 's what *you* are!' (He got that idea out of a duet he sings with Almiry Berry.) Now I'd like to know whether that ain't pleasanter than 't is to have a man do all the shed 'n' barn work up smart, and then set round the stove looking as doleful as a last year's bird's nest? Take my advice, Miss Hollis: get a good provider if you can, but anyhow try to find you a husband that'll keep on courting a little now and then, when he ain't too busy; it smooths things consid'able round the house.

"There, I got so int'rested in what I was saying, I've went on and finished the carnation, and some of the stem, too. Now what comes next? Why, the thing that happened next, of course, and that was little Jot.

"I'll work in a bud on my rose and one on Lovey's, and my bud'll be made of Jot's first trousers. The goods ain't very appropriate for a rosebud, but it'll have to do, for the idee is the most important thing in this rug. When I put him into pants, I hadn't any cloth in the house, and it was such bad going Jot couldn't get to Wareham to buy me anything; so I made 'em out of an old gray cashmere skirt, and lined 'em with flannel."

"Buds are generally the same color as the roses, aren't they?" ventured Priscilla.

"I don't care if they be," said Diadema obstinately. "What's to hender this bud's bein' grafted on? Mrs. Granger was as black as an Injun, but the little Granger children were all red-headed, for they took after their father. But I don't know; you've kind o' got me out o' conceit with it. I s'pose I could have taken a piece of his baby blanket; but the moths never et a mite o' that, and it's too good to cut up. There's one thing I can do: I can make the bud up with a long stem, and have it growing right up alongside of mine,—would you?"

"No, it must be stalk of your stalk, bone of your bone, flesh of your flesh, so to speak. I agree with you, the idea is the first thing. Besides, the gray is a very light shade, and I dare say it will look like a bluish white."

"I'll try it and see, but I wish to the land the moths *had* eat the pinning-blanket, and then I could have used it. Lovey worked the scallops on the aidge for me. My grief! what int'rest she took in my baby clothes! Little Jot was born at Thanksgiving time, and she come over from Skowhegan, where Reuben was settled pastor of his first church. I shall never forget them two weeks to the last day of my life. There was deep snow on the ground. I had that chamber there, with the door opening into the setting-room. Mother and father Bascom kep' out in the dining-room and kitchen, where the work was going on, and Lovey and the baby and me had the front part of the house to ourselves, with Jot coming in on tiptoe, heaping up wood in the fireplace so 't he 'most roasted us out. He don't forget his chores in time o' sickness.

"I never took so much comfort in all my days. Jot got one of the Billings girls to come over and help in the housework, so 't I could lay easy 's long as I wanted to; and I never had such a rest before nor since. There ain't any heaven in the book o' Revelations that 's any better than them two weeks was. I used to lay quiet in my good feather bed, fingering the pattern of my best crochet quilt, and looking at the fire-light shining on Lovey and the baby. She 'd hardly leave him in the cradle a minute. When I did n't want him in bed with me, she 'd have him in her lap. Babies are common enough to most folks, but Lovey was diff'rent. She 'd never had any experience with children, either, for we was the youngest in our family; and it wa'n't long before we come near being the oldest, too, for mother buried seven of us before she went herself. Anyway, I never saw nobody else look as she done when she held my baby. I don't mean nothing blasphemious when I say 't was for all the world like your photograph of Mary, the mother of Jesus.

"The nights come in early, so it was 'most dark at four o'clock. The little chamber was so peaceful! I could hear Jot rattling the milk-pails, but I'd draw a deep breath o' comfort, for I knew the milk would be strained and set away without my stepping foot to the floor. Lovey used to set by the fire, with a tall candle on the light-stand behind her, and a little white knit cape over her shoulders. She had the pinkest cheeks, and the longest eyelashes, and a mouth like a little red buttonhole; and when she bent over the baby, and sung to him,—though his ears wa'n't open, I guess for his eyes wa'n't,—the tears o' joy used to rain down my cheeks. It was pennyrial hymns she used to sing mostly, and the one I remember best was

"Daniel's wisdom may I know,

Stephen's faith and spirit show;

John's divine communion feel,

Moses' meekness, Joshua's zeal,

Run like the unwearied Paul,

Win the day and conquer all.

"Mary's love may I possess,

Lydia's tender-heartedness,

Peter's fervent spirit feel,

James's faith by works reveal,

Like young Timothy may I

Every sinful passion fly.'

"'Oh Diademy,' she 'd say, 'you was always the best, and it 's nothing more 'n right the baby should have come to you. P'r'aps God will think I'm good enough some time; and if he does, Diademy, I'll offer up a sacrifice every morning and every evening. But I'm afraid,' says she, 'he thinks I can't stand any more happiness, and be a faithful follower of the cross. The Bible says we 've got to wade through fiery floods before we can enter the kingdom. I don't hardly know how Reuben and I are going to find any way to wade through; we're both so happy, they 'd have to be consid'able hot before we took notice,' says she, with the dimples all breaking out in her cheeks.

"And that was true as gospel. She thought everything Reuben done was just right, and he thought everything she done was just right. There wa'n't nobody else; the world was all Reuben 'n' all Lovey to them. If you could have seen her when she was looking for him to come from Skowhegan! She used to watch at the attic window; and when she seen him at the foot of the hill she'd up like a squirrel, and run down the road without stopping for anything but to throw a shawl over her head. And Reuben would ketch her up as if she was a child, and scold her for not putting a hat on, and take her under his coat coming up the hill. They was a sight for the neighbors, I must confess, but it wa'n't one you could hardly disapprove of, neither. Aunt Hitty said it was tempting Providence and couldn't last, and God would visit his wrath on 'em for making idols of sinful human flesh.

"She was right one way,—it didn't last; but nobody can tell me God was punishing of 'em for being too happy. I guess he 'ain't got no objection to folks being happy here below, if they don't forget it ain't the whole story.

"Well, I must mark in a bud on Lovey's stalk now, and I'm going to make it of her baby's long white cloak. I earned the money for it myself, making coats, and put four yards of the finest cashmere into it; for three years after little Jot was born I went over to Skowhegan to help Lovey through her time o' trial. Time o' trial! I thought I was happy, but I didn't know how to be as happy as Lovey did; I wa'n't made on that pattern.

"When I first showed her the baby (it was a boy, same as mine), her eyes shone like two evening stars. She held up her weak arms, and gathered the little bundle o' warm flannen into 'em; and when she got it close she shut her eyes and moved her lips, and I knew she was taking her lamb to the altar and offering it up as a sacrifice. Then Reuben come in. I seen him give one look at the two dark heads laying close together on the white piller, and then go down on his knees by the side of the bed. 'T wa'n't no place for me; I went off, and left 'em together. We didn't mistrust it then, but they only had three days more of happiness, and I'm glad I give 'em every minute."

The room grew dusky as twilight stole gently over the hills of Pleasant River. Priscilla's lip trembled; Diadema's tears fell thick and fast on the white rosebud, and she had to keep wiping her eyes as she followed the pattern.

"I ain't said as much as this about it for five years," she went on, with a tell-tale quiver in her voice, "but now I've got going I can't stop. I'll have to get the weight out o' my heart somehow.

"Three days after I put Lovey's baby into her arms the Lord called her home. 'When I prayed so hard for this little new life, Reuben,' says she holding the baby as if she could never let it go, 'I didn't think I'd got to give up my own in place of it; but it's the first fiery flood we've had, dear, and though it burns to my feet I'll tread it as brave as I know how.'

"She didn't speak a word after that; she just faded away like a snowdrop, hour by hour. And Reuben and I stared at one another in the face as if we was dead instead of her, and we went about that house o' mourning like sleepwalkers for days and says, not knowing whether we et or slept, or what we done.

"As for the baby, the poor little mite didn't live many hours after its mother, and we buried 'em together. Reuben and I knew what Lovey would have liked. She gave her life for the baby's, and it was a useless sacrifice, after all. No, it wa'n't neither; it *could*n't have been! You needn't tell me God'll let such sacrifices as that come out useless! But anyhow, we had one coffin for 'em both, and I opened Lovey's arms and laid the baby in 'em. When Reuben and I took our last look, we thought she seemed more 'n ever like Mary, the mother of Jesus. There never was another like her, and there never will be. 'Nonesuch,' Reuben used to call her."

There was silence in the room, broken only by the ticking of the old clock and the tinkle of a distant cowbell. Priscilla made an impetuous movement, flung herself down by the basket of rags, and buried her head in Diadema's gingham apron.

"Dear Mrs. Bascom, don't cry. I'm sorry, as the children say."

"No, I won't more 'n a minute. Jot can't stand it to see me give way. You go and touch a match to the kitchen fire, so 't the kettle will be boiling, and I'll have a minute to myself. I don't know what the neighbors would think to ketch me crying over my drawing-in frame; but the spell's over now, or 'bout over, and when I can muster up courage I'll take the rest of the baby's cloak and put a border of white everlastings round the outside of the rug. I'll always mean the baby's birth and Lovey's death to me; but the flowers will remind me it 's life everlasting for both of 'em, and so it's the most comforting end I can think of."

It was indeed a beautiful rug when it was finished and laid in front of the sofa in the fore-room. Diadema was very choice of it. When company was expected she removed it from its accustomed place, and spread it in a corner of the room where no profane foot could possibly tread on it. Unexpected callers were managed by a different method. If they seated themselves on the sofa, she would fear they did not "set easy" or "rest comfortable" there, and suggest their moving to the stuffed chair by the window. The neighbors thought this solicitude merely another sign of Diadema's "p'ison neatness," excusable in this case as there was so much white in the new rug.

The fore-room blinds were ordinarily closed, and the chillness of death pervaded the sacred apartment; but on great occasions, when the sun was allowed to penetrate the thirty-two tiny panes of glass in each window, and a blaze was lighted in the fire-place, Miss Hollis would look in as she went upstairs, and muse a moment over the pathetic little romance of rags, the story of two lives worked into a bouquet of old-fashioned posies, whose gay tints were brought out by a setting of sombre threads. Existence had gone so quietly in this remote corner of the world that all its important events, babyhood, childhood, betrothal, marriage, motherhood, with all their mysteries of love and life and death, were chronicled in this narrow space not two yards square.

Diadema came in behind the little school-teacher one afternoon.

"I cal'late," she said, "that being kep' in a dark room, and never being tread on, it will last longer 'n I do. If it does, Priscilla, you know that white crepe shawl of mine I wear to meeting hot Sundays: that would make a second row of everlastings round the border. You could piece out the linings good and smooth on the under side, draw in the white flowers, and fill 'em round with black to set 'em off. The rug would be han'somer than ever then, and the story—would be finished."

A VILLAGE STRADIVARIUS.

I.

"Goodfellow, Puck and goblins,
Know more than any book.
Down with your doleful problems,
And court the sunny brook.
The south-winds are quick-witted,
The schools are sad and slow,
The masters quite omitted
The lore we care to know."

Emerson's April.

"Find the 317th page, Davy, and begin at the top of the right-hand column."

The boy turned the leaves of the old instruction book obediently, and then began to read in a sing-song, monotonous tone:—

"'One of Pag-pag'"—

"Pag-a-ni-ni's."

"'One of Paggernyner's' (I wish all the fellers in your stories didn't have such tough old names!) 'most dis-as-ter-ous triumphs he had when playing at Lord Holland's.' (Who was Lord Holland, uncle Tony?) 'Some one asked him to im-pro-vise on the violin the story of a son who kills his father, runs a-way, becomes a highway-man, falls in love with a girl who will not listen to him; so he leads her to a wild country site, suddenly jumping with her from a rock into an a-b-y-double-s'"—

"Abyss."

"'—a—rock—into—an—abyss, were they disappear forever. Paggernyner listened quietly, and when the story was at an end he asked that all the lights should be distinguished.'"

"Look closer, Davy."

"'Should be extinguished. He then began playing, and so terrible was the musical in-ter-pre-ta-tion of the idea which had been given him that several of the ladies fainted, and the sal-salon-s*a*lon, when relighted, looked like a battle-field.' Cracky! Wouldn't you like to have been there, uncle Tony? But I don't believe anybody ever played that way, do you?"

"Yes," said the listener, dreamily raising his sightless eyes to the elm-tree that grew by the kitchen door. "I believe it, and I can hear it myself when you read the story to me. I feel that the secret of everything in the world that is beautiful, or true, or terrible, is hidden in the strings of my violin, Davy, but only a master can draw it from captivity."

"You make stories on your violin, too, uncle Tony, even if the ladies don't faint away in heaps, and if the kitchen doesn't look like a battle-field when you 've finished. I'm glad it doesn't, for my part, for I should have more housework to do than ever."

"Poor Davy! you couldn't hate housework any worse if you were a woman; but it is all done for to-day. Now paint me one of your pictures, laddie; make me see with your eyes."

The boy put down the book and leaped out of the open door, barely touching the old millstone that served for a step. Taking a stand in the well-worn path, he rested his hands on his hips, swept the landscape with the glance of an eagle, and began like a young improvisator:—

"The sun is just dropping behind Brigadier Hill."

"What color is it?"

"Red as fire, and there isn't anything near it,—it 's almost alone in the sky; there 's only teenty little white feather clouds here and there. The bridge looks as if it was a silver string tying the two sides of the river together. The water is pink where the sun shines into it. All the leaves of the trees are kind of swimming in the red light,—I tell you, nunky, just as if I was looking through red glass. The weather vane on Squire Bean's barn dazzles so the rooster seems to be shooting gold arrows into the river. I can see the tip top of Mount Washington where the peak of its snow-cap touches the pink sky. The hen-house door is open. The chickens are all on their roost, with their heads cuddled under their wings."

"Did you feed them?"

The boy clapped his hand over his mouth with a comical gesture of penitence, and dashed into the shed for a panful of corn, which he scattered over the ground, enticing the sleepy fowls by insinuating calls of "Chick, chick, chick, chick! *Come,* biddy, biddy, biddy, biddy! *Come,* chick, chick, chick, chick, chick!"

The man in the doorway smiled as over the misdemeanor of somebody very dear and lovable, and rising from his chair felt his way to a corner shelf, took down a box, and drew from it a violin swathed in a silk bag. He removed the covering with reverential hands. The tenderness of the face was like that of a young mother dressing or undressing her child. As he fingered the instrument his hands seemed to have become all eyes. They wandered caressingly over the polished surface as if enamored of the perfect thing that they had created, lingering here and there with rapturous tenderness on some special beauty,—the graceful arch of the neck, the melting curves of the cheeks, the delicious swell of the breasts.

When he had satisfied himself for the moment, he took the bow, and lifting the violin under his chin, inclined his head fondly toward it and began to play.

The tune at first seemed muffled, but had a curious bite, that began in distant echoes, but after a few minutes' the playing grew firmer and clearer, ringing out at last with velvety richness and strength until the atmosphere was satiated with harmony. No more ethereal note ever flew out of a bird's throat than Anthony Croft set free from this violin, his *liebling*, his "swan song," made in the year he had lost his eyesight.

Anthony Croft had been the only son of his mother, and she a widow. His boyhood had been exactly like that of all the other boys in Edgewood, save that he hated school a trifle more, if possible, than any of the others; though there was a unanimity of aversion in this matter that surprised and wounded teachers and parents.

The school was the ordinary "deestrick" school of that time; there were not enough scholars for what Cyse Higgins called a "degraded" school. The difference between Anthony and the other boys lay in the reason as well as the degree of his abhorrence.

He had come into the world a naked, starving human soul; he longed to clothe himself, and he was hungry and ever hungrier for knowledge; but never within the four walls of the village schoolhouse could he get hold of one fact that would yield him its secret sense, one glimpse of clear light that would shine in upon the "darkness which may be felt" in his mind, one thought or word that would feed his soul.

The only place where his longings were ever stilled, where he seemed at peace with himself, where he understood what he was made for, was out of doors in the woods. When he should have been poring over the sweet, palpitating mysteries of the multiplication table, his vagrant gaze was always on the open window near which he sat. He could never study when a fly buzzed on the window-pane; he was always standing on the toes of his bare feet, trying to locate and understand the buzz that puzzled him. The book was a mute, soulless thing that had no relation to his inner world of thought and feeling.

He turned ever from the dead seven-times-six to the mystery of life about him.

He was never a special favorite with his teachers; that was scarcely to be expected. In his very early years, his pockets were gone through with every morning when he entered the school door, and the contents, when confiscated, would comprise a jew's-harp, a bit of catgut, screws whittled out of wood, tacks, spools, pins, and the like. But when robbed of all these he could generally secrete a piece of elastic, which, when put between his teeth and stretched to its utmost capacity, would yield a delightful twang when played upon with the forefinger. He could also fashion an interesting musical instrument in his desk by means of spools and catgut and bits of broken glass. The chief joy of his life was an old tuning-fork that the teacher of the singing school had given him, but, owing to the degrading and arbitrary censorship of pockets that prevailed, he never dared bring it into the schoolroom. There were ways, however, of evading inexorable law and circumventing base injustice. He hid the precious thing under a thistle just outside the window. The teacher had sometimes a brief season of apathy on hot afternoons, when she was hearing the primer class read, "*I see a pig. The pig is big. The big pig can dig;*" which stirring in phrases were always punctuated by the snores of the Hanks baby, who kept sinking down on his fat little legs in the line and giving way to slumber during the lesson. At such a moment Anthony slipped out of the window and snapped the tuning-fork several times,—just enough to save his soul from death,—and then slipped in again. He was caught occasionally, but not often; and even when he was, there were mitigating circumstances, for he was generally put under the teacher's desk for punishment. It was a dark, close, sultry spot, but when he was well seated, and had grown tied of looking at the triangle of elastic in the teacher's congress boot, and tired of wishing it was his instead of hers, he would tie one end of a bit of thread to the button of his gingham shirt, and, carrying it round his left ear several times, make believe he was Paganini languishing in prison and playing on a violin with a single string.

As he grew older there was no marked improvement, and Tony Croft was by general assent counted the laziest boy in the village. That he was lazy in certain matters merely because he was in a frenzy of industry to pursue certain others had nothing to do with the case, of course.

If any one had ever given him a task in which he could have seen cause working to effect, in which he could have found by personal experiment a single fact that belonged to him, his own by divine right of discovery, he would have counted labor or study all joy.

He was one incarnate Why and How, one brooding wonder and interrogation point. "Why does the sun drive away the stars? Why do the leaves turn red and gold? What makes the seed swell in the earth? From whence comes the life hidden in the egg under the bird's breast? What holds the moon in the sky? Who regulates her shining? Who moves the wind? Who made me, and what am I? Who, why, how whither? If I came from God but only lately, teach me his lessons first, put me into vital relation with life and law, and then give me your dead signs and equivalents for real things, that I may learn more and more, and ever more and ever more."

There was no spirit in Edgewood bold enough to conceive that Tony learned anything in the woods, but as there was never sufficient school money to keep the village seat of learning open more than half the year the boy educated himself at the fountain head of wisdom, and knowledge of the other half. His mother, who owned him for a duckling hatched from a hen's egg, and was never quite sure he would not turn out a black sheep and a crooked stick to boot, was obliged to confess that Tony had more useless information than any boy in the village. He knew just where to find the first Mayflowers, and would bring home the waxen beauties when other people had scarcely begun to think about the spring. He could tell where to look for the rare fringed gentian, the yellow violet, the Indian pipe. There were clefts in the rocks of the Indian Cellar where, when every one else failed, he could find harebells and columbines.

When his tasks were done, and the other boys were amusing themselves each in his own way, you would find Tony lying flat on the pine needles in the woods, listening to the notes of the wild birds, and imitating them patiently, til you could scarcely tell which was boy and which was bird; and if you could, the birds couldn't, for many a time he coaxed the bobolinks and thrushes to perch on the low boughs above his head and chirp to him as if he were a feathered brother. There was nothing about the building of nests with which he was not familiar. He could have taken hold and helped if the birds had not been so shy, and if he had had beak and claw instead of clumsy fingers. He would sit near a beehive for hours without moving, or lie prone in the sandy road, under the full glare of the sun, watching the ants acting out their human comedy; sometimes surrounding a favorite hill with stones, that the comedy might not be turned into a tragedy by a careless footfall. The cottage on the river road grew more and more to resemble a museum and herbarium as the years went by, and the Widow Croft's weekly house-cleaning was a matter that called for the exercise of Christian grace.

Still, Tony was a good son, affectionate, considerate, and obedient. His mother had no idea that he would ever be able, or indeed willing, to make a living; but there was a forest of young timber growing up, a small hay farm to depend upon, and a little hoard that would keep him out of the poorhouse when she died and left him to his own devices. It never occurred to her that he was in any way remarkable. If he were difficult to understand, it reflected more upon his eccentricity than upon her density. What was a woman to do with a boy of twelve who, when she urged him to drop the old guitar he was taking apart and hurry off to school, cried, "Oh, mother! when there is so much to learn in this world, it is wicked, wicked to waste time in school."

About this period Tony spent hours in the attic arranging bottles and tumblers into a musical scale. He also invented an instrument made of small and great, long and short pins, driven into soft board to different depths, and when the widow passed his door on the way to bed she invariable saw this barbaric thing locked up to the boy's breast, for he often played himself to sleep with it.

At fifteen he had taken to pieces and put together again, strengthened, soldered, tinkered, mended, and braced every accordion, guitar, melodeon, dulcimer, and fiddle in Edgewood, Pleasant River, and the neighboring villages. There was a little money to be earned in this way, but very little, as people in general regarded this "tinkering" as a pleasing diversion in which they could indulge him without danger. As an example of this attitude, Dr. Berry's wife's melodeon had lost two stops, the pedals had severed connection with the rest of the works, it wheezed like an asthmatic, and two black keys were missing. Anthony worked more than a week on its rehabilitation, and received in return Mrs. Berry's promise that the doctor would pull a tooth for him some time! This, of course, was a guerdon for the future, but it seemed pathetically distant to the lad who had never had a toothache in his life. He had to plead with Cyse Higgins for a week before that prudent young farmer would allow him to touch his five-dollar fiddle. He obtained permission at last only because by offering to give Cyse his calf in case he spoiled the violin. "That seems square," said Cyse doubtfully, "but after all, you can't play on a calf!" "Neither will your fiddle give milk, if you keep it long enough," retorted Tony; and this argument was convincing.

So great was his confidence in Tony's skill that Squire Bean trusted his father's violin to him, one that had been bought in Berlin seventy years before. It had been hanging on the attic wall for a half century, so that the back was split in twain, the sound-post lost, the neck and the tailpiece cracked. The lad took it home, and studied it for two whole evenings before the open fire. The problem of restoring it was quite beyond his abilities. He finally took the savings of two summers' "blueberry money" and walked sixteen miles to Portland, where he bought a book called The Practical Violinist. The Supplement proved to be a mine of wealth. Even the headings appealed to his imagination and intoxicated him with their suggestions,—On Scraping, Splitting, and Repairing Violins, Violin Players, Great Violinists, Solo Playing, etc.; and at the very end a Treatise on the Construction, Preservation, Repair, and Improvement of the Violin, by Jacob Augustus Friedheim, Instrument Maker to the Court of the Archduke of Weimar.

There was a good deal of moral advice in the preface that sadly puzzled the boy, who was always in a condition of chronic amazement at the village disapprobation of his favorite fiddle. That the violin did not in some way receive the confidence enjoyed by other musical instruments, he perceived from various paragraphs written by the worthy author of The Practical Violinist, as for example:—

"Some very excellent Christian people hold a strong prejudice against the violin because they have always known it associated with dancing and dissipation. Let it be understood that your violin is 'converted,' and such an obligation will no longer lie against it. ... Many delightful hours may be enjoyed by a young man, if he has obtained a respectable knowledge of his instrument, who otherwise would find the time hang heavy on his hands; or, for want of some better amusement, would frequent the dangerous and destructive paths of vice and be ruined forever. ... I am in hopes, therefore, my dear young pupil, that your violin will occupy your attention at just those very times when, if you were immoral or dissipated, you would be at the grogshop, gaming-table, or among vicious females. Such a use of the violin, notwithstanding the prejudices many hold against it, must contribute to virtue, and furnish abundance of innocent and entirely unobjectionable amusement. These are the views with which I hope you have adopted it, and will continue to cherish and cultivate it."

II.

"There is no bard in all the choir,

....

Not one of all can put in verse,

Or to this presence could rehearse

The sights and voices ravishing

The boy knew on the hills in spring,

When pacing through the oaks he heard

Sharp queries of the sentry-bird,

The heavy grouse's sudden whir,

The rattle of the kingfisher."

Emerson's Harp.

Now began an era of infinite happiness, of days that were never long enough, of evenings when bedtime came all too soon. Oh that there had been some good angel who would have taken in hand Anthony Croft the boy, and, training the powers that pointed so unmistakably in certain directions, given to the world the genius of Anthony Croft, potential instrument maker to the court of St. Cecilia; for it was not only that he had the fingers of a wizard; his ear caught the faintest breath of harmony or hint of discord, as

"Fairy folk a-listening
Hear the seed sprout in the spring,
And for music to their dance
Hear the hedge-rows wake from trance;
Sap that trembles into buds
Sending little rhythmic floods
Of fairy sound in fairy ears.
Thus all beauty that appears
Has birth as sound to finer sense
And lighter-clad intelligence."

As the universe is all mechanism to one man, all form and color to another, so to Anthony Croft the world was all melody. Notwithstanding all these gifts and possibilities, the doctor's wife advised the Widow Croft to make a plumber of him, intimating delicately that these freaks of nature, while playing no apparent part in the divine economy, could sometimes be made self-supporting.

The seventeenth year of his life marked a definite epoch in his development. He studied Jacob Friedheim's treatise until he knew the characteristics of all the great violin models, from the Amatis, Hieronymus, Antonius, and Nicolas, to those of Stradivarius, Guarnerius, and Steiner.

It was in this year, also, that he made a very precious discovery. While browsing in the rubbish in Squire Bean's garret to see if he could find the missing sound-post of the old violin, he came upon a billet of wood wrapped in cloth and paper. When unwrapped, it was plainly labeled "Wood from the Bean Maple at Pleasant Point; the biggest maple in York County, and believed to be one of the biggest in the State of Maine." Anthony found that the oldest inhabitant of Pleasant River remembered the stump of the tree, and that the boys used to jump over it and admire its proportions whenever they went fishing at the Point. The wood, therefore, was perhaps eighty or ninety years old. The squire agreed willingly that it should be used to mend the old violin, and told Tony he should have what was left for himself. When, by careful calculation, he found that the remainder would make a whole violin, he laid it reverently away for another twenty years, so that he should be sure it had completed its century of patient waiting for service, and falling on his knees by his bedside said, "I thank Thee, Heavenly Father, for this precious gift, and I promise from this moment to gather the most beautiful wood I can find, and lay it by where it can be used some time to make perfect violins, so that if any creature as poor and helpless as I am needs the wherewithal to do good work, I shall have helped him as Thou hast helped me." And according to his promise so he did, and the pieces of richly curled maple, of sycamore, and of spruce began to accumulate. They were cut from the sunny side of the trees, in just the right season of the year, split so as to have a full inch thickness towards the bark, and a quarter inch towards the heart. They were then laid for weeks under one of the falls in Wine Brook, where the musical tinkle, tinkle of the stream fell on the wood already wrought upon by years of sunshine and choruses of singing birds.

This boy, toiling not alone for himself, but with full and conscious purpose for posterity also, was he not worthy to wear the mantle of Antonius Stradivarius?

"That plain white-aproned man who stood at work Patient and accurate full fourscore years, Cherished his sight and touch by temperance, And since keen sense is love of perfectness, Made perfect violins, the needed paths For inspiration and high mastery."

And as if the year were not full enough of glory, the school-teacher sent him a book with a wonderful poem in it.

That summer's teaching had been the freak of a college student, who had gone back to his senior year strengthened by his experience of village life. Anthony Croft, who was only three or four years his junior, had been his favorite pupil and companion.

"How does Tony get along?" asked the Widow Croft when the teacher came to call.

"Tony? Oh, I can't teach him anything."

Tears sprang to the mother's eyes.

"I know he ain't much on book learning," she said apologetically, "but I'm bound he don't make you no trouble in deportment."

"I mean," said the school-teacher gravely, "that I can show him how to read a little Latin and do a little geometry, but he knows as much in one day as I shall ever know in a year."

Tony crouched by the old fireplace in the winter evenings, dropping his knife or his compasses a moment to read aloud to his mother, who sat in the opposite corner knitting:—

"Of old Antonio Stradivari,—him
Who a good quarter century and a half ago
Put his true work in the brown instrument,
And by the nice adjustment of its frame
Gave it responsive life, continuous
With the master's finger-tips, and perfected
Like them by delicate rectitude of use."

The mother listened with painful intentness. "I like the sound of it," she said, "but I can't hardly say I take in the full sense."

"Why mother," said the lad, in a rare moment of self-expression, "you know the poetry says he cherished his sight and touch by temperance; that an idiot might see a straggling line and be content, but he had an eye that winced at false work, and loved the true. When it says his finger-tips were perfected by delicate rectitude of use, I think it means doing everything as it is done in heaven, and that anybody who wants to make a perfect violin must keep his eye open to all the beautiful things God has made, and his ear open to all the music he has put into the world, and then never let his hands touch a piece of work that is crooked or straggling or false, till, after years and years of rightness, they are fit to make a violin like the squire's, a violin that can say everything, a violin that an angel wouldn't be ashamed to play on."

Do these words seem likely ones to fall from the lips of a lad who had been at the tail of his class ever since his primer days? Well, Anthony was seventeen now, and he was "educated," in spite of sorry recitations,—educated, the Lord knows how! Yes, in point of fact the Lord does know how! He knows how the drill and pressure of the daily task, still more the presence of the high ideal, the inspiration working from within, how these educate us.

The blind Anthony Croft sitting in the kitchen doorway had seemingly missed the heights of life he might have trod, and had walked his close on fifty years through level meadows of mediocrity, a witch in every finger-tip waiting to be set to work, head among the clouds, feet stumbling, eyes and ears open to hear God's secret thought; seeing and hearing it, too, but lacking force to speak it forth again; for while imperious genius surmounts all obstacles, brushes laws and formulas from its horizon, and with its own free soul sees its "path and the outlets of the sky," potential genius forever needs an angel of deliverance to set it free.

Poor Anthony Croft, or blessed Anthony Croft, I know not which,—God knows! Poor he certainly was, yet blessed after all. "One thing I do," said Paul. "One thing I do," said Anthony. He was not able to realize his ideals, but he had the "angel aim" by which he idealized his reals.

O waiting heart of God! how soon would thy kingdom come if we all did our allotted tasks, humble or splendid, in this consecrated fashion!

III.

"Therein I hear the Parcae reel

The threads of man at their humming wheel,

The threads of life and power and pain,

So sweet and mournful falls the strain."

Emerson's Harp.

Old Mrs. Butterfield had had her third stroke of paralysis, and died of a Sunday night. She was all alone in her little cottage on the river bank, with no neighbor nearer than Croft's, and nobody there but a blind man and a small boy. Everybody had told her it was foolish to live alone in a house on the river road, and everybody was pleased in a discreet and chastened fashion of course, that it had turned out exactly as they had predicted.

Aunt Mehitable Tarbox was walking up to Milliken's Mills, with her little black reticule hanging over her arm, and noticing that there was no smoke coming out of the chimney, and that the hens were gathered about the kitchen door clamoring for their breakfast, she thought it best to stop and knock. No response followed the repeated blows from her hard knuckles. She then tapped smartly on Mrs. Butterfield's bedroom window with her thimble finger. This proving of no avail, she was obliged to pry open the kitchen shutter, split open a mosquito netting with her shears, and crawl into the house over the sink. This was a considerable feat for a somewhat rheumatic elderly lady, but this one never grudged trouble when she wanted to find out anything.

When she discovered that her premonitions were correct, and that old Mrs. Butterfield was indeed dead, her grief at losing a pleasant acquaintance was largely mitigated by her sense of importance at being first on the spot, and chosen by Providence to take command of the situation. There were no relations in the village; there was no woman neighbor within a mile: it was therefore her obvious Christian duty not only to take charge of the remains, but to conduct such a funeral as the remains would have wished for herself.

The fortunate Vice-President suddenly called upon by destiny to guide the ship of state, the general who sees a possible Victoria Cross in a hazardous engagement, can have a faint conception of aunt Hitty's feeling on this momentous occasion. Funerals were the very breath of her life. There was no ceremony, either of public or private import, that, to her mind, approached a funeral in real satisfying interest. Yet, with distinct talent in this direction, she had always been "cabined, cribbed, confined" within hopeless limitations. She had assisted in a secondary capacity at funerals in the families of other people, but she would have reveled in personally conducted ones. The members of her own family stubbornly refused to die, however, even the distant connections living on and on to a ridiculous old age; and if they ever did die, by reason of a falling roof, shipwreck, or conflagration, they generally died in Texas or Iowa, or some remote State where aunt Hitty could not follow the hearse in the first carriage. This blighted ambition was a heart sorrow of so deep and sacred a character that she did not even confess it to "Si," as her appendage of a husband was called.

Now at last her chance for planning a funeral had come. Mrs. Butterfield had no kith or kin save her niece, Lyddy Ann, who lived in Andover, or Lawrence, or Haverhill Massachusetts,—aunt Hitty couldn't remember which, and hoped nobody else could. The niece would be sent for when they found out where she lived; meanwhile the funeral could not be put off.

She glanced round the house preparatory to locking it up and starting to notify Anthony Croft. She would just run over and talk to him about ordering the coffin; then she could attend to all other necessary preliminaries herself. The remains had been well-to-do, and there was no occasion for sordid economy, so aunt Hitty determined in her own mind to have the latest fashion in everything, including a silver coffin plate. The Butterfield coffin plates were a thing to be proud of. They had been sacredly preserved for years and years, and the entire collection—numbering nineteen in all had been framed, and adorned the walls of the deceased lady's best room. They were not of solid silver, it is true, but even so it was a matter of distinction to have belonged to a family that could afford to have nineteen coffin plates of any sort.

Aunt Hitty planned certain dramatic details as she walked town the road to Croft's. It came to her in a burst of inspiration that she would have two ministers: one for the long prayer, and one for the short prayer and the remarks. She hoped that Elder Weeks would be adequate in the latter direction. She knew she couldn't for the life of her think of anything interesting about Mrs. Butterfield, save that she possessed nineteen coffin plates, and brought her hens to Edgewood every summer for their health; but she had heard Elder Weeks make a moving discourse out of less than that. To be sure, he needed priming, but she was equal to that. There was Ivory Brown's funeral: how would that have gone on if it hadn't been for her? Wasn't the elder ten minutes late, and what would his remarks have amounted to without her suggestions? You might almost say she was the author of the discourse, for she gave him all the appropriate ideas. As she had helped him out of the wagon she had said: "Are you prepared? I thought not; but there's no time to lose. Remember there are aged parents; two brothers living, one railroading in Spokane Falls, the other clerking in Washington, D. C. Don't mention the Universalists,—there's ben two in the fam'ly; nor insanity,—there 's ben one o' them. The girl in the corner by the clock is the one that the remains has been keeping comp'ny with. If you can make some genteel allusions to her, it'll be much appreciated by his folks."

As to the long prayer, she knew that the Rev. Mr. Ford could be relied on to pray until aunt Becky Burnham should twitch him by the coat tails. She had done it more than once. She had also, on one occasion, got up and straightened his ministerial neckerchief, which he had gradually "prayed" around his saintly neck until it was behind the right ear.

These plans proved so fascinating to aunt Hitty that she walked quite half a mile beyond Croft's, and was obliged to retrace her steps. She conceived bands of black alpaca for the sleeves and hats of the pallbearers, and a festoon of the same over the front gate, if there should be any left over. She planned the singing by the choir. There had been no real choir-singing at any funeral in Edgewood since the Rev. Joshua Beckwith had died. She would ask them to open with—

Rebel mourner, cease your weepin'.

You too must die.

This was a favorite funeral hymn. The only difficulty would be in keeping aunt Becky Burnham from pitching it in a key where nobody but a soprano skylark, accustomed to warble at a great height, could possibly sing it. It was generally given at the grave, when Elder Weeks officiated; but it never satisfied aunt Hitty, because the good elder always looked so unpicturesque when he threw a red bandanna handkerchief over his head before beginning the twenty-seven verses. After the long prayer, she would have Almira Berry give for a solo—

This gro-o-oanin' world 's too dark and

dre-e-ar for the saints' e - ter - nal rest,

This hymn, if it did not wholly reconcile one to death, enabled one to look upon life with sufficient solemnity. It was a thousand pities, she thought, that the old hearse was so shabby and rickety, and that Gooly Eldridge, who drove it, would insist on wearing a faded peach-blow overcoat. It was exasperating to think of the public spirit at Egypt, and contrast it with the state of things at Pleasant River. In Egypt they had sold the old hearse house for a sausage shop, and now they were having hearse sociables every month to raise money for a new one.

All these details flew through aunt Hitty's mind in fascinating procession. There shouldn't be "a hitch" anywhere. There had been a hitch at her last funeral, but she had been only an assistant there. Matt Henderson had been struck by lightning at the foot of Squire Bean's old nooning tree, and certain circumstances combined to make the funeral one of unusual interest, so much so that fat old Mrs. Potter from Deerwander created a sensation at the cemetery. She was so anxious to get where she could see everything to the best advantage that she crowded too near the bier, stepped on the sliding earth, and pitched into the grave. As she weighed over two hundred pounds, and was in a position of some disadvantage, it took five men to extricate her from the dilemma, and the operation made a long and somewhat awkward break in the religious services. Aunt Hitty always said of this catastrophe, "If I'd 'a' ben Mis' Potter, I'd 'a' ben so mortified I believe I'd 'a' said, 'I wa'n't plannin' to be buried, but now I'm in here I declare I'll stop!'"

Old Mrs. Butterfield's funeral was not only voted an entire success by the villagers, but the seal of professional approval was set upon it by an undertaker from Saco, who declared that Mrs. Tarbox could make a handsome living in the funeral line anywhere. Providence, who always assists those who assist themselves, decreed that the niece Lyddy Ann should not arrive until the aunt was safely buried; so, there being none to resist her right or grudge her the privilege aunt Hitty, for the first time in her life, rode in the next buggy to the hearse. Si, in his best suit, a broad weed and weepers, drove Cyse Higgins's black colt, and aunt Hitty was dressed in deep mourning, with the Widow Buzzell's crape veil over her face, and in her hand a palmleaf fan tied with a black ribbon. Her comment to Si, as she went to her virtuous couch that night, was: "It was an awful dry funeral, but that was the only flaw in it. It would 'a' ben perfect if there' ben anybody to shed tears. I come pretty nigh it myself, though I ain't no relation, when Elder Weeks said, 'You'll go round the house, my sisters, and Mis' Butterfield won't be there; you'll go int' the orchard, and Mis' Butterfield won't be there; you'll go int' the barn and Mis' Butterfield won't be there; you'll go int' the shed, and Mis' Butterfield won't be there; you'll go int' the hencoop, and Mis' Butterfield won't be there!' That would 'a' drawed tears from a stone most, 'specially sence Mis' Butterfield set such store by her hens."

And this is the way that Lyddy Butterfield came into her kingdom, a little lone brown house on the river's brim. She had seen it only once before when she had driven out from Portland, years ago, with her aunt. Mrs. Butterfield lived in Portland, but spent her summers in Edgewood on account of her chickens. She always explained that the country was dreadful dull for her, but good for the hens; they always laid so much better in the winter time.

Lyddy liked the place all the better for its loneliness. She had never had enough of solitude, and this quiet home, with the song of the river for company, if one needed more company than chickens and a cat, satisfied all her desires, particularly as it was accompanied by a snug little income of two hundred dollars a year, a meagre sum that seemed to open up mysterious avenues of joy to her starved, impatient heart.

When she was a mere infant, her brother was holding her on his knee before the great old-fashioned fireplace heaped with burning logs. A sudden noise startled him, and the crowing, restless baby gave an unexpected lurch, and slipped, face downward, into the glowing embers. It was a full minute before the horror-stricken boy could extricate the little creature from the cruel flame that had already done its fatal work. The baby escaped with her life, but was disfigured forever. As she grew older, the gentle hand of time could not entirely efface the terrible scars. One cheek was wrinkled and crimson, while one eye and the mouth were drawn down pathetically. The accident might have changed the disposition of any child, but Lyddy chanced to be a sensitive, introspective bit of feminine humanity, in whose memory the burning flame was never quenched. Her mother, partly to conceal her own wounded vanity, and partly to shield the timid, morbid child, kept her out of sight as much as possible; so that at sixteen, when she was left an orphan, she had lived almost entirely in solitude.

She became, in course of time, a kind of general nursery governess in a large family of motherless children. The father was almost always away from home; his sister kept the house, and Lyddy stayed in the nursery, bathing the brood and putting them to bed, dressing them in the morning, and playing with them in the safe privacy of the back garden or the open attic. They loved her, disfigured as she was, for the child despises mere externals, and explores the heart of things to see whether it be good or evil,—but they could never induce her to see strangers, nor to join any gathering of people.

The children were grown and married now, and Lyddy was nearly forty when she came into possession of house and lands and fortune; forty, with twenty years of unexpended feeling pent within her. Forty, that is rather old to be interesting, but age is a relative matter. Haven't you seen girls of four-and-twenty who have nibbled and been nibbled at ever since they were sixteen, but who have neither caught anything nor been caught? They are old, if you like, but Lyddy was forty and still young, with her susceptibilities cherished, not dulled, and with all the "language of passion fresh and rooted as the lovely leafage about a spring."

IV.

"He shall daily joy dispense
Hid in song's sweet influence."

Emerson's Merlin.

Lyddy had very few callers during her first month as a property owner in Edgewood. Her appearance would have been against her winning friends easily in any case, even if she had not acquired the habits of a recluse. It took a certain amount of time, too, for the community to get used to the fact that old Mrs. Butterfield was dead, and her niece Lyddy Ann living in the cottage on the river road. There were numbers of people who had not yet heard that old Mrs. Butterfield had bought the house from the Thatcher boys, and that was fifteen years ago; but this was not strange, for, notwithstanding aunt Hitty's valuable services in disseminating general information, there was a man living on the Bonny Eagle road who was surprised to hear that Daniel Webster was dead, and complained that folks were not so long-lived as they used to be.

Aunt Hitty thought Lyddy a Goth and a Vandal because she took down the twenty silver coffin plates and laid them reverently away. "Mis' Butterfield would turn in her grave," she said, "if she knew it. She ain't much of a housekeeper, I guess," she went on, as she cut over Dr. Berry's old trousers into briefer ones for Tommy Berry. "She gives considerable stuff to her hens that she'd a sight better heat over and eat herself, in these hard times when the missionary societies can't hardly keep the heathen fed and clothed and warmed—no, I don't mean warmed, for most o' the heathens live in hot climates, somehow or 'nother. My back door's jest opposite hers; it's across the river, to be sure, but it's the narrer part, and I can see everything she does as plain as daylight. She washed a Monday, and she ain't taken her clothes in yet, and it's Thursday. She may be bleachin' of 'em out, but it looks slack. I said to Si last night I should stand it till 'bout Friday,—seein' 'em lay on the grass there, but if she didn't take 'em in then, I should go over and offer to help her. She has a fire in the settin'-room 'most every night, though we ain't had a frost yet; and as near's I can make out, she's got full red curtains hangin' up to her windows. I ain't sure, for she don't open the blinds in that room till I get away in the morning, and she shuts 'em before I get back at night. Si don't know red from green, so he's useless in such matters. I'm going home late to-night, and walk down on that side o' the river, so't I can call in after dark and see what makes her house light up as if the sun was settin' inside of it."

As a matter of fact, Lyddy was reveling in house-furnishing of a humble sort. She had a passion for color. There was a red-and-white straw matting on the sitting-room floor. Reckless in the certain possession of twenty dollars a month, she purchased yards upon yards of turkey red cotton; enough to cover a mattress for the high-backed settle, for long curtains at the windows, and for cushions to the rockers. She knotted white fringes for the table covers and curtains, painted the inside of the fireplace red, put some pots, of scarlet geraniums on the window-sills, filled newspaper rack with ferns and tacked it over an ugly spot in the wall, edged her work-basket with a tufted trimming of scarlet worsted, and made an elaborate photograph case of white crash and red cotton that stretched the entire length of the old-fashioned mantelshelf, and held pictures of Mr. Reynolds, Miss Elvira Reynolds, George, Susy, Anna, John, Hazel, Ella, and Rufus Reynolds, her former charges. When all this was done, she lighted a little blaze on the hearth, took the red curtains from their hands, let them fall gracefully to the floor, and sat down in her rocking-chair, reconciled to her existence for absolutely the first time in her forty years.

I hope Mrs. Butterfield was happy enough in Paradise to appreciate and feel Lyddy's joy. I can even believe she was glad to have died, since her dying could bring such content to any wretched living human soul. As Lydia sat in the firelight, the left side of her poor face in shadow, you saw that she was distinctly harmonious. Her figure, clad in plain black-and-white calico dress, was a graceful, womanly one. She had beautifully sloping shoulders and a sweet wrist. Her hair was soft and plentiful, and her hands were fine, strong, and sensitive. This possibility of rare beauty made her scars and burns more pitiful, for if a cheap chrome has smirch across its face, we think it a matter of no moment, but we deplore the smallest scratch or blur on any work of real art.

Lydia felt a little less bitter and hopeless about life when she sat in front of her own open fire, after her usual twilight walk. It was her habit to wander down the wooded road after her simple five-o'clock supper, gatherings ferns or goldenrod or frost flowers for her vases; and one night she heard, above the rippling of the river, the strange, sweet, piercing sound of Anthony Croft's violin.

She drew nearer, and saw a middle-aged man sitting in the kitchen doorway, with a lad of ten or twelve years leaning against his knees. She could tell little of his appearance, save that he had a high forehead, and hair that waved well back from it in rather an unusual fashion. He was in his shirt-sleeves, but the gingham was scrupulously clean, and he had the uncommon refinement of a collar and necktie. Out of sight herself, Lyddy drew near enough to hear; and this she did every night without recognizing that the musician was blind. The music had a curious effect upon her. It was a hitherto unknown influence in her life, and it interpreted her, so to speak, to herself. As she sat on the bed of brown pine needles, under a friendly tree, her head resting against its trunk, her eyes half closed, the tone of Anthony's violin came like a heavenly message to a tired, despairing soul. Remember that in her secluded life she had heard only such harmony as Elvira Reynolds evoked from her piano or George Reynolds from his flute, and the Reynolds temperament was distinctly inartistic.

Lyddy lived through a lifetime of emotion in these twilight concerts. Sometimes she was filled with an exquisite melancholy from which there was no escape; at others, the ethereal purity of the strain stirred her heart with a strange, sweet vision of mysterious joy; joy that she had never possessed, would never possess; joy whose bare existence she never before realized. When the low notes sank lower and lower with their soft wail of delicious woe, she bent forward into the dark, dreading that something would be lost in the very struggle of listening; then, after a, pause, a pure human tone would break the stillness, and soaring, bird-like, higher and higher, seem to mount to heaven itself, and, "piercing its starry floors," lift poor scarred Lydia's soul to the very grates of infinite bliss. In the gentle moods that stole upon her in those summer twilights she became a different woman, softer in her prosperity than she had ever been in her adversity; for some plants only blossom in sunshine. What wonder if to her the music and the musician became one? It is sometimes a dangerous thing to fuse the man and his talents in this way; but it did no harm here, for Anthony Croft was his music, and the music was Anthony Croft. When he played on his violin, it was as if the miracle of its fashioning were again enacted; as if the bird on the quivering bough, the mellow sunshine streaming through the lattice of green leaves, the tinkle of the woodland stream, spoke in every tone; and more than this, the hearth-glow in whose light the patient hands had worked, the breath of the soul bending itself in passionate prayer for perfection, these, too, seemed to have wrought their blessed influence on the willing strings until the tone was laden with spiritual harmony. One might indeed have sung of this little red violin—that looked to Lyddy, in the sunset glow, as if it were veneered with rubies—all that Shelley sang of another perfect instrument:—

"The artist who this viol wrought

To echo all harmonious thought,

Fell'd a tree, while on the steep

The woods were in their winter sleep,

Rock'd in that repose divine
Of the wind-swept Apennine;
And dreaming, some of Autumn past,
And some of Spring approaching fast,
And some of April buds and showers,
And some of songs in July bowers,
And all of love; and so this tree—
O that such our death may be!—
Died in sleep, and felt no pain,
To live in happier form again."

The viol "whispers in enamoured tone:"—
"Sweet oracles of woods and dells,
And summer windy ill sylvan cells;..
The clearest echoes of the hills,
The softest notes of falling rills,
The melodies of birds and bees,
The murmuring of summer seas,
And pattering rain, and breathing dew,
And airs of evening; all it knew....
—All this it knows, but will not tell
To those who cannot question well
The spirit that inhabits it;...
But, sweetly as its answers will
Flatter hands of perfect skill,
It keeps its highest, holiest tone
For one beloved Friend alone."

Lyddy heard the violin and the man's voice as he talked to the child,—heard them night after night; and when she went home to the little brown house to light the fire on the hearth and let down the warm red curtains, she fell into sweet, sad reveries; and when she blew out her candle for the night, she fell asleep and dreamed new dreams, and her heart was stirred with the rustling of new-born hopes that rose and took wing like birds startled from their nests.

V.

"Nor scour the seas, nor sift mankind,
A poet or a friend to find:
Behold, he watches at the door!
Behold his shadow on the floor!"

Emerson's Saadi.

Lyddy Butterfield's hen turkey was of a roving disposition. She had never appreciated her luxurious country quarters in Edgewood, and was seemingly anxious to return to the modest back yard in her native city. At any rate, she was in the habit of straying far from home, and the habit was growing upon her to such an extent that she would even lead her docile little gobblers down to visit Anthony Croft's hens and share their corn.

Lyddy had caught her at it once, and was now pursuing her to that end for the second time. She paused in front of the house, but there were no turkeys to be seen. Could they have wandered up the hill road,—the discontented, "traipsing," exasperating things? She started in that direction, when she heard a crash in the Croft kitchen, and then the sound of a boy's voice coming from an inner room,—a weak and querulous voice, as if the child were ill.

She drew nearer, in spite of her dread of meeting people, or above all of intruding, and saw Anthony Croft standing over the stove, with an expression of utter helplessness on his usually placid face. She had never really seen him before in the daylight, and there was something about his appearance that startled her. The teakettle was on the floor, and a sea of water was flooding the man's feet, yet he seemed to be gazing into vacancy. Presently he stooped, and fumbled gropingly for the kettle. It was too hot to be touched with impunity, and he finally left it in a despairing sort of way, and walked in the direction of a shelf, from under which a row of coats was hanging. The boy called again in a louder and more insistent tone, ending in a whimper of restless pain. This seemed to make the man more nervous than ever. His hands went patiently over and over the shelf, then paused at each separate nail.

"Bless the poor dear!" thought Lyddy. "Is he trying to find his hat, or what is he trying to do? I wonder if he is music mad?" and she drew still nearer the steps.

At this moment he turned and came rapidly toward the door. She looked straight in his face. There was no mistaking it: he was blind. The magician who had told her through his violin secrets that she had scarcely dreamed of, the wizard who had set her heart to throbbing and aching and longing as it had never throbbed and ached and longed before, the being who had worn a halo of romance and genius to her simple mind, was stone-blind! A wave of impetuous anguish, as sharp and passionate as any she had ever felt for her own misfortunes, swept over her soul at the spectacle of the man's helplessness. His sightless eyes struck her like a blow. But there was no time to lose. She was directly in his path: if she stood still he would certainly walk over her, and if she moved he would hear her, so, on the spur of the moment, she gave a nervous cough and said, "Good-morning, Mr. Croft."

He stopped short. "Who is it?" he asked.

"I am—it is—I am—your new neighbor," said Lyddy, with a trembling attempt at cheerfulness.

"Oh, Miss Butterfield! I should have called up to see you before this if it hadn't been for the boy's sickness. But I am a good-for-nothing neighbor, as you have doubtless heard. Nobody expects anything of me."

("Nobody expects anything of me." Her own plaint, uttered in her own tone!)

"I don't know about that," she answered swiftly. "You've given me, for one, a great deal of pleasure with your wonderful music. I often hear you as you play after supper, and it has kept me from being lonesome. That isn't very much, to be sure."

"You are fond of music, then?"

"I didn't know I was; I never heard any before," said Lyddy simply; "but it seems to help people to say things they couldn't say for themselves, don't you think so? It comforts me even to hear it, and I think it must be still more beautiful to make it."

Now, Lyddy Ann Butterfield had no sooner uttered this commonplace speech than the reflection darted through her mind like a lightning flash that she had never spoken a bit of her heart out like this in all her life before. The reason came to her in the same flash: she was not being looked at; her disfigured face was hidden. This man, at least, could not shrink, turn away, shiver, affect indifference, fix his eyes on hers with a fascinated horror, as others had done. Her heart was divided between a great throb of pity and sympathy for him and an irresistible sense of gratitude for herself. Sure of protection and comprehension, her lovely soul came out of her poor eyes and sat in the sunshine. She spoke her mind at ease, as we utter sacred things sometimes under cover of darkness.

"You seem to have had an accident; what can I do to help you?" she asked.

"Nothing, thank you. The boy has been sick for some days, but he seems worse since last night. Nothing is in its right place in the house, so I have given up trying to find anything, and am just going to Edgewood to see if somebody will help me for a few days."

"Uncle Tony! Uncle To-ny! where are you? Do give me another drink, I'm so hot!" came the boy's voice from within.

"Coming, laddie! I don't believe he ought to drink so much water, but what can I do? He is burning up with fever."

"Now look here, Mr. Croft," and Lydia's tone was cheerfully decisive. "You sit down in that rocker, please, and let me command the ship for a while. This is one of the cases where a woman is necessary. First and foremost, what were you hunting for?"

"My hat and the butter," said Anthony meekly, and at this unique combination they both laughed. Lyddy's laugh was particularly fresh, childlike, and pleased; one that would have astonished the Reynolds children. She had seldom laughed heartily since little Rufus had cried and told her she frightened him when she twisted her face so.

"Your hat is in the wood-box, and I'll find the butter in the twinkling of an eye, though why you want it now is more than—My patience, Mr. Croft, your hand is burned to a blister!"

"Don't mind me. Be good enough to look at the boy and tell me what ails him; nothing else matters much."

"I will with pleasure, but let me ease you a little first. Here's a rag that will be just the thing," and Lyddy, suiting the pretty action to the mendacious worn, took a good handkerchief from her pocket and tore it in three strips, after spreading it with tallow from a candle heated over the stove. This done, she hound up the burned hand skillfully, and, crossing the dining-room, disappeared within the little chamber door beyond. She came out presently, and said half hesitatingly, "Would you—mind going out in the orchard for an hour or so? You seem to be rather in the way here, and I should like the place to myself, if you'll excuse me for saying so. I'm ever so much more capable than Mrs. Buck; won't you give me a trial, sir? Here's your violin and your hat. I'll call you if you can help or advise me."

"But I can't let a stranger come in and do my housework," he objected. "I can't, you know, though I appreciate your kindness all the same."

"I am your nearest neighbor, and your only one, for that matter," said Lyddy firmly; "its nothing more than right that I should look after that sick child, and I must do it. I haven't got a thing to do in my own house. I am nothing but a poor lonely old maid, who's been used to children all her life, and likes nothing better than to work over them."

A calm settled upon Anthony's perturbed spirit, as he sat under the apple-trees and heard Lyddy going to and fro in the cottage. "She isn't any old maid," he thought; "she doesn't step like one; she has soft shoes and a springy walk. She must be a very handsome woman, with a hand like that; and such a voice! I knew the moment she spoke that she didn't belong in this village."

As a matter of fact, his keen ear had caught the melody in Lyddy's voice, a voice full of dignity, sweetness, and reserve power. His sense of touch, too, had captured the beauty of her hand, and held it in remembrance,—the soft palm, the fine skin, supple fingers, smooth nails, and firm round wrist. These charms would never have been noted by any seeing man in Edgewood, but they were revealed to Anthony Croft while Lyddy, like the good Samaritan, bound up his wounds. It is these saving stars that light the eternal darkness of the blind.

Lyddy thought she had met her Waterloo when, with arms akimbo, she gazed about the Croft establishment, which was a scene of desolation for the moment. Anthony's cousin from Bridgton was in the habit of visiting him every two months for a solemn house-cleaning, and Mrs. Buck from Pleasant River came every Saturday and Monday for baking and washing. Between times Davy and his uncle did the housework together; and although it was respectably done, there was no pink-and-white daintiness about it, you may be sure.

Lyddy came out to the apple-trees in about an hour, laughing a little nervously as she said, "I'm sorry to have taken a mean advantage of you, Mr. Croft, but I know everything you've got in your house, and exactly where it is. I couldn't help it, you see, when I was making things tidy. It would do you good to see the boy. His room was too light, and the flies were devouring him. I swept him and dusted him, put on clean sheets and pillow slips, sponged him with bay rum, brushed his hair, drove out the flies, and tacked a green curtain up to the window. Fifteen minutes after he was sleeping like a kitten. He has a sore throat and considerable fever. Could you—can you—at least, will you, go up to my house on an errand?"

"Certainly I can. I know it inside and out as well as my own."

"Very good. On the clock shelf in the sitting-room there is a bottle of sweet spirits of nitre; it's the only bottle there, so you can't make any mistake. It will help until the doctor comes. I wonder you didn't send for him yesterday?"

"Davy wouldn't have him," apologized his uncle.

"Wouldn't he?" said Lyddy with cheerful scorn. "He has you under pretty good control, hasn't he? But children are unmerciful tyrants."

"Couldn't you coax him into it before you go home?" asked Anthony in a wheedling voice.

"I can try; but it isn't likely I can influence him, if you can't. Still, if we both fail, I really don't see what 's to prevent our sending for the doctor in spite of him. He is as weak as a baby, you know, and can't sit up in bed: what could he do? I will risk the consequences, if you will!"

There was a note of such amiable and winning sarcasm in all this, such a cheery, invincible courage, such a friendly neighborliness and cooperation, above all such a different tone from any he was accustomed to hear in Edgewood, that Anthony Croft felt warmed through to the core.

As he walked quickly along the road, he conjured up a vision of autumn beauty from the few hints nature gave even to her sightless ones on this glorious morning,—the rustle of a few fallen leaves under his feet, the clear wine of the air, the full rush of the swollen river, the whisking of the squirrels in the boughs, the crunch of their teeth on the nuts, the spicy odor of the apples lying under the trees. He missed his mother that morning more than he had missed her for years. How neat she was, how thrifty, how comfortable, and how comforting! His life was so dreary and aimless; and was it the best or the right one for Davy, with his talent and dawning ambition? Would it not be better to have Mrs. Buck live with them altogether, instead of coming twice a week, as heretofore? No; he shrank from that with a hopeless aversion born of Saturday and Monday dinners in her company. He could hear her pour her coffee into the saucer; hear the scraping of the cup on the rim, and know that she was setting it sloppily down on the cloth. He could remember her noisy drinking, the weight of her elbow on the table, the creaking of her calico dress under the pressure of superabundant flesh. Besides, she had tried to scrub his favorite violin with sapolio. No, anything was better than Mrs. Buck as a constancy.

He took off his hat unconsciously as he entered Lyddy's sitting-room. A gentle breeze blew one of the full red curtains towards him till it fluttered about his shoulders like a frolicsome, teasing hand. There was a sweet, pungent odor of pine boughs, a canary sang in the window, the clock was trimmed with a blackberry vine; he knew the prickles, and they called up to his mind the glowing tints he had loved so well. His sensitive hand, that carried a divining rod in every finger-tip, met a vase on the shelf, and, traveling upward, touched a full branch of alder berries tied about with a ribbon. The ribbon would be red; the woman who arranged this room would make no mistake; for in one morning Anthony Croft had penetrated the secret of Lyddy's true personality, and in a measure had sounded the shallows that led to the depths of her nature.

Lyddy went home at seven o'clock that night rather reluctantly. The doctor had said Mr. Croft could sit up with the boy unless he grew much worse, and there was no propriety in her staying longer unless there was danger.

"You have been very good to me," Anthony said gravely, as he shook her hand at parting,—"very good."

They stood together on the doorstep. A distant bell, called to evening prayer-meeting; the restless murmur of the river and the whisper of the wind in the pines broke the twilight stillness. The long, quiet day together, part of it spent by the sick child's bedside, had brought the two strangers curiously near to each other.

"The house hasn't seemed so sweet and fresh since my mother died," he went on, as he dropped her hand, "and I haven't had so many flowers and green things in it since I lost my eyesight."

"Was it long ago?"

"Ten years. Is that long?"

"Long to bear a burden."

"I hope you know little of burden-bearing?"

"I know little else."

"I might have guessed it from the alacrity with which you took up Davy's and mine. You must be very happy to have the power to make things straight and sunny and wholesome; to breathe your strength into helplessness such as mine. I thank you, and I envy you. Good-night."

Lyddy turned on her heel without a word; her mind was beyond and above words. The sky seemed to have descended upon, enveloped her, caught her up into its heaven, as she rose into unaccustomed heights of feeling, like Elijah in his chariot of fire. She very happy! She with power, power to make things straight and sunny and wholesome! She able to breathe strength into helplessness, even a consecrated, Godsmitten helplessness like his! She not only to be thanked, but envied!

Her house seemed strange to her that night. She went to bed in the dark, dreading even the light of a candle; and before she turned down her counterpane she flung herself on her knees, and poured out her soul in a prayer that had been growing, waiting, and waited for, perhaps, for years:—

"O Lord, I thank Thee for health and strength and life. I never could do it before, but I thank Thee to-night for life on any terms. I thank Thee for this home; for the chance of helping another human creature, stricken like myself; for the privilege of ministering to a motherless child. Make me to long only for the beauty of holiness, and to be satisfied if I attain to it. Wash my soul pure and clean, and let that be the only mirror in which I see my face. I have tried to be useful. Forgive me if it always seemed so hard and dreary a life. Forgive me if I am too happy because for one short day I have really helped in a beautiful way, and found a friend who saw, because he was blind, the real me underneath; the me that never was burned by the fire; the me that isn't disfigured, unless my wicked discontent has done it; the me that has lived on and on and on, starving to death for the friendship and sympathy and love that come to other women. I have spent my forty years in the wilderness, feeding on wrath and bitterness and tears. Forgive me, Lord, and give me one more vision of the blessed land of Canaan, even if I never dwell there."

VI.

"Nor less the eternal poles
Of tendency distribute souls.
There need no vows to bind
Whom not each other seek, but find."

Emerson's Celestial Love.

Davy's sickness was a lingering one. Mrs. Buck came for two or three hours a day, but Lyddy was the self-installed angel of the house; and before a week had passed the boy's thin arms were around her neck, his head on her loving shoulder, and his cheek pressed against hers. Anthony could hear them talk, as he sat in the kitchen busy at his work. Musical instruments were still brought him to repair, though less frequently than of yore, and he could still make many parts of violins far better than his seeing competitors. A friend and pupil sat by his side in the winter evenings and supplemented his weakness, helping and learning alternately, while his blind master's skill filled him with wonder and despair. The years of struggle for perfection had not been wasted; and though the eye that once detected the deviation of a hair's breadth could no longer tell the true from the false, yet nature had been busy with her divine work of compensation. The one sense stricken with death, she poured floods of new life and vigor into the others. Touch became something more than the stupid, empty grasp of things we seeing mortals know, and in place of the two eyes he had lost he now had ten in every fingertip. As for odors, let other folks be proud of smelling musk and lavender, but let him tell you by a quiver of the nostrils the various kinds of so-called scentless flowers, and let him bend his ear and interpret secrets that the universe is ever whispering to us who are pent in partial deafness because, forsooth, we see.

He often paused to hear Lydia's low, soothing tones and the boy's weak treble. Anthony had said to him once, "Miss Butterfield is very beautiful, isn't she, Davy? You haven't painted me a picture of her yet. How does she look?"

Davy was stricken at first with silent embarrassment. He was a truthful child, but in this he could no more have told the whole truth than he could have cut off his hand. He was knit to Lyddy by every tie of gratitude and affection. He would sit for hours with his expectant face pressed against the windowpane, and when he saw her coming down the shady road he was filled with a sense of impending comfort and joy.

"NO," he said hesitatingly, "she isn't pretty, nunky, but she's sweet and nice and dear, Everything on her shines, it's so clean; and when she comes through the trees, with her white apron and her purple calico dress, your heart jumps, because you know she's going to make everything pleasant. Her hair has a pretty wave in it, and her hand is soft on your forehead; and it's most worth while being sick just to have her in the house."

Meanwhile, so truly is "praise our fructifying sun," Lydia bloomed into a hundred hitherto unsuspected graces of mind and heart and speech. A sly sense of humor woke into life, and a positive talent for conversation, latent hitherto because she had never known any one who cared to drop a plummet into the crystal springs of her consciousness. When the violin was laid away, she would sit in the twilight, by Davy's sofa, his thin hand in hers, and talk with Anthony about books and flowers and music, and about the meaning of life, too,—its burdens and mistakes, and joys and sorrows; groping with him in the darkness to find a clue to God's purposes.

Davy had long afternoons at Lyddy's house as the autumn grew into winter. He read to her while she sewed rags for a new sitting-room carpet, and they played dominoes and checkers together in the twilight before supper time,— suppers that were a feast to the boy, after Mrs. Buck's cookery. Anthony brought his violin sometimes of an evening, and Almira Berry, the next neighbor on the road to the Mills, would drop in and join the little party. Almira used to sing Auld Robin Gray, What Will You Do, Love, and Robin Adair, to the great enjoyment of everybody; and she persuaded Lyddy to buy the old church melodeon, and learn to sing alto in Oh, Wert Thou in the Cauld Blast, Gently, Gently Sighs the Breeze, and I know a Bank. Nobody sighed for the gayeties and advantages of a great city when, these concerts being over, Lyddy would pass crisp seedcakes and raspberry shrub, doughnuts and cider, or hot popped corn and molasses candy.

"But there, she can afford to," said aunt Hitty Tarbox; "she's pretty middlin' wealthy for Edgewood. And it's lucky she is, for she 'bout feeds that boy o' Croft's. No wonder he wants her to fill him up, after six years of the Widder Buck's victuals. Aurelia Buck can take good flour and sugar, sweet butter and fresh eggs, and in ten strokes of her hand she can make 'em into something the very hogs 'll turn away from. I declare, it brings the tears to my eyes sometimes when I see her coming out of Croft's Saturday afternoons, and think of the stone crocks full of nasty messes she's left behind her for that innocent man and boy to eat up.... Anthony goes to see Miss Butterfield consid'able often. Of course it's awstensibly to walk home with Davy, or do an errand or something, but everybody knows better. She went down to Croft's pretty nearly every day when his cousin from Bridgton come to house-clean. She suspicioned something, I guess. Anyhow, she asked me if Miss Butterfield's two hundred a year was in gov'ment bonds. Anthony's eyesight ain't good, but I guess he could make out to cut cowpons off.... It would be strange if them two left-overs should take an' marry each other; though, come to think of it, I don't know's 't would neither. He's blind, to be sure, and can't see her scarred face. It's a pity she ain't deef, so't she can't hear his everlastin' fiddle. She's lucky to get any kind of a husband; she's too humbly to choose. I declare, she reminds me of a Jack-o'-lantern, though if you look at the back of her, or see her in meetin' with a thick veil on, she's about the best appearin' woman in Edgewood.... I never see anybody stiffen up as Anthony has. He had me make him three white shirts and three gingham ones, with collars and cuffs on all of 'em. It seems as if six shirts at one time must mean something out o' the common!"

Aunt Hitty was right; it did mean something out of the common. It meant the growth of an all-engrossing, grateful, divinely tender passion between two love-starved souls. On the one hand, Lyddy, who though she had scarcely known the meaning of love in all her dreary life, yet was as full to the brim of all sweet, womanly possibilities of loving and giving as any pretty woman; on the other, the blind violin-maker, who had never loved any woman but his mother, and who was in the direst need of womanly sympathy and affection.

Anthony Croft, being ministered unto by Lyddy's kind hands, hearing her sweet voice and her soft footstep, saw her as God sees, knowing the best; forgiving the worst, like God, and forgetting it, still more like God, I think.

And Lyddy? There is no pen worthy to write of Lyddy. Her joy lay deep in her heart like a jewel at the bottom of a clear pool, so deep that no ripple or ruffle on the surface could disturb the hidden treasure. If God had smitten these two with one hand, he had held out the other in tender benediction.

There had been a pitiful scene of unspeakable solemnity when Anthony first told Lyddy that he loved her, and asked her to be his wife. He had heard all her sad history by this time, though not from her own lips, and his heart went out to her all the more for the heavy cross that had been laid upon her. He had the wit and wisdom to put her affliction quite out of the question, and allude only to her sacrifice in marrying a blind man, hopelessly and helplessly dependent on her sweet offices for the rest of his life, if she, in her womanly mercy, would love him and help him bear his burdens.

When his tender words fell upon Lyddy's dazed brain she sank beside his chair, and, clasping his knees, sobbed: "I love you, I cannot help loving you, I cannot help telling you I love you! But you must hear the truth; you have heard it from others, but perhaps they softened it. If I marry you, people will always blame me and pity you. You would never ask me to be your wife if you could see my face; you could not love me an instant if you were not blind."

"Then I thank God unceasingly for my infirmity," said Anthony Croft, as he raised her to her feet.

Anthony and Lyddy Croft sat in the apple orchard, one warm day in late spring.

Anthony's work would have puzzled a casual on-looker. Ten stout wires were stretched between two trees, fifteen or twenty feet apart, and each group of five represented the lines of the musical staff. Wooden bars crossed the wires at regular intervals, dividing the staff into measures. A box with many compartments sat on a stool beside him, and this held bits of wood that looked like pegs, but were in reality whole, half, quarter, and eighth notes, rests, flats, sharps, and the like. These were cleft in such a way that he could fit them on the wires almost as rapidly as his musical theme came to him, and Lyddy had learned to transcribe with pen and ink the music she found in wood and wire, He could write only simple airs in this way, but when he played them on the violin they were transported into a loftier region, such genius lay in the harmony, the arabesque, the delicate lacework of embroidery with which the tune was inwrought; now high, now low, now major, now minor, now sad, now gay, with the one thrilling, haunting cadence recurring again and again, to be watched for, longed for, and greeted with a throb of delight.

Davy was reading at the window, his curly head buried in a well-worn Shakespeare opened at Midsummer Night's Dream. Lyddy was sitting under her favorite pink apple-tree, a mass of fragrant bloom, more beautiful than Aurora's morning gown. She was sewing; lining with snowy lawn innumerable pockets in a square basket that she held in her lap. The pockets were small, the needles were fine, the thread was a length of cobweb. Everything about the basket was small except the hopes that she was stitching into it; they were so great that her heart could scarcely hold them. Nature was stirring everywhere. The seeds were springing in the warm earth. The hens were clucking to their downy chicks just out of the egg. The birds were flying hither and thither in the apple boughs, and there was one little home of straw so hung that Lyddy could look into it and see the patient mother brooding her nestlings. The sight of her bright eyes, alert for every sign of danger, sent a rush of feeling through Lyddy's veins that made her long to clasp the little feathered mother to her own breast.

A sweet gravity and consecration of thought possessed her, and the pink blossoms falling into her basket were not more delicate than the rose-colored dreams that flushed her soul.

Anthony put in the last wooden peg, and taking up his violin called, "Davy, lad, come out and tell me what this means!"

Davy was used to this; from a wee boy he had been asked to paint the changing landscape of each day, and to put into words his uncle's music.

Lyddy dropped her needle, the birds stopped to listen, and Anthony played.

"It is this apple orchard in May time," said Davy; "it is the song of the green things growing, isn't it?"

"What do you say, dear?" asked Anthony, turning to his wife.

Love and hope had made a poet of Lyddy. "I think Davy is right," she said. "It is a dream of the future, the story of all new and beautiful things growing out of the old. It is full of the sweetness of present joy, but there is promise and hope in it besides. It is like the Spring sitting in the lap of Winter, and holding a baby Summer in her bosom."

Davy did not quite understand this, though he thought it pretty; but Lyddy's husband did, and when the boy went back to his books, he took his wife in his arms and kissed her twice,—once for herself, and then once again.

THE EVENTFUL TRIP OF THE MIDNIGHT CRY.

In the little villages along the Saco River, in the year 1850 or thereabouts, the arrival and departure of the stage-coach was the one exciting incident of the day. It did not run on schedule time in those days, but started from Limington or Saco, as the case might be, at about or somewhere near a certain hour, and arrived at the other end of the route whenever it got there. There were no trains to meet (the railway popularly known as the "York and Yank'em" was not built till 1862); the roads were occasionally good and generally bad; and thus it was often dusk, and sometimes late in the evening, when the lumbering vehicle neared its final destination and drew up to the little post-offices along the way. However late it might be, the village postmaster had to be on hand to receive and open the mailbags; after which he distributed the newspapers and letters in a primitive set of pine pigeon-holes on the wall, turned out the loafers, "banked up" the fire, and went home to bed.

"Life" Lane was a jolly good fellow,—just the man to sit on the box seat and drive the three horses through ruts and "thank-you-ma'ams," slush and mud and snow. There was a perennial twinkle in his eye, his ruddy cheeks were wrinkled with laughter, and he had a good story forever on the tip of his tongue. He stood six feet two in his stockings (his mother used to say she had the longest Life of any woman in the State o' Maine); his shoulders were broad in proportion, and his lungs just the sort to fill amply his noble chest. Therefore, when he had what was called in the vernacular "turrible bad goin'," and when any other stage-driver in York County would have shrunk into his muffler and snapped and snarled on the slightest provocation, Life Lane opened his great throat when he passed over the bridges at Moderation or Bonny Eagle, and sent forth a golden, sonorous "Yo ho! halloo!" into the still air. The later it was and the stormier it was, the more vigor he put into the note, and it was a drowsy postmaster indeed who did not start from his bench by the fire at the sound of that ringing halloo. Thus the old stage-coach, in Life Lane's time, was generally called "The Midnight Cry," and not such a bad name either, whether the term was derisively applied because the stage was always late; or whether Life's "Yo ho!" had caught the popular fancy.

There was a pretty girl in Pleasant River (and, alas! another in Bonny Eagle) who went to bed every night with the chickens, but stayed awake till she heard first the rumble of heavy wheels on a bridge, then a faint, bell-like tone that might have come out of the mouth of a silver horn; whereupon she blushed as if it were an offer of marriage, and turned over and went to sleep.

If the stage arrived in good season, Life would have a few minutes to sit on the loafers' beach beside the big open fire; and what a feature he was, with his tales culled from all sorts of passengers, who were never so fluent as when sitting beside him "up in front!" There was a tallow dip or two, and no other light save that of the fire. Who that ever told a story could wish a more inspiring auditor than Jacob Bean, a literal, honest old fellow who took the most vital interest in every detail of the stories told, looking upon their heroes and their villains as personal friends or foes. He always sat in one corner of the fireplace, poker in hand, and the crowd tacitly allowed him the role of Greek chorus. Indeed, nobody could have told a story properly without Jake Bean's parentheses and punctuation marks poked in at exciting junctures.

"That 's so every time!" he would say, with a lunge at the forestick. "I'll bate he was glad then!" with another stick flung on in just the right spot. "Golly! but that served 'em right!" with a thrust at the backlog.

The New England story seemed to flourish under these conditions: a couple of good hard benches in a store or tavern, where you could not only smoke and chew but could keep on your hat (there was not a man in York County in those days who could say anything worth hearing with his hat off); the blazing logs to poke; and a cavernous fireplace into which tobacco juice could be neatly and judiciously directed. Those were good old times, and the stage-coach was a mighty thing when school children were taught to take off their hats and make a bow as the United States mail passed the old stage tavern.

Life Lane's coaching days were over long before this story begins, but the Midnight Cry was still in pretty fair condition, and was driven ostensibly by Jeremiah Todd, who lived on the "back-nippin'" road from Bonny Eagle to Limington.

When I say ostensibly driven, I but follow the lead of the villagers, who declared that, though Jerry held the reins, Mrs. Todd drove the stage, as she drove everything else. As a proof of this lady's strong individuality, she was still generally spoken of as "the Widder Bixby," though she had been six years wedded to Jeremiah Todd. The Widder Bixby, then, was strong, self-reliant, valiant, indomitable. Jerry Todd was, to use his wife's own characterization, so soft you could stick a cat's tail into him without ruffling the fur. He was always alluded to as "the Widder Bixby's husband;" but that was no new or special mortification, for he had been known successively as Mrs. Todd's youngest baby, the Widder Todd's only son, Susan Todd's brother, and, when Susan Todd's oldest boy fought at Chapultepec, William Peck's uncle.

The Widder Bixby's record was far different. She was the mildest of the four Stover sisters of Scarboro, and the quartette was supposed to have furnished more kinds of temper than had ever before come from one household. When

Peace, the eldest, was mad, she frequently kicked the churn out of the kitchen door, cream and all,—and that lost her a husband.

Love, the second, married, and according to local tradition once kicked her husband all the way up Foolscap Hill with a dried cod-fish. Charity, the third, married too,—for the Stovers of Scarboro were handsome girls, but she got a fit mate in her spouse. She failed to intimidate him, for he was a foeman worthy of her steel; but she left his bed and board, and left in a manner that kept up the credit of the Stover family of Scarboro.

They had had a stormy breakfast one morning before he started to Portland with a load of hay. "Good-by," she called, as she stood in the door, "you've seen the last of me!" "No such luck!" he said, and whipped up his horse. Charity baked a great pile of biscuits, and left them on the kitchen table with a pitcher of skimmed milk. (She wouldn't give him anything to complain of, not she!) She then put a few clothes in a bundle, and, tying on her shaker, prepared to walk to Pleasant River, twelve miles distant. As she locked the door and put the key in its accustomed place under the mat, a pleasant young man drove up and explained that he was the advance agent of the Sypher's Two-in-One Menagerie and Circus, soon to appear in that vicinity. He added that he should be glad to give her five tickets to the entertainment if she would allow him to paste a few handsome posters on that side of her barn next the road; that their removal was attended with trifling difficulty, owing to the nature of a very superior paste invented by himself; that any small boy, in fact, could tear them off in an hour, and be well paid by the gift of a ticket.

The devil entered into Charity (not by any means for the first time), and she told the man composedly that if he would give her ten tickets he might paper over the cottage as well as the barn, for they were going to tear it down shortly and build a larger one. The advance agent was delighted, and they passed a pleasant hour together; Charity holding the paste-pot, while the talkative gentleman glued six lions and an elephant on the roof, a fat lady on the front door, a tattooed man between the windows, living skeletons on the blinds, and ladies insufficiently clothed in all the vacant spaces and on the chimneys. Nobody went by during the operation, and the agent remarked, as he unhitched his horse, that he had never done a neater job. "Why, they'll come as far to see your house as they will to the circus!" he exclaimed.

"I calculate they will," said Charity, as she latched the gate and started for Pleasant River.

I am not telling Charity Stover's story, so I will only add that the bill-poster was mistaken in the nature of his paste, and greatly undervalued its adhesive properties.

The temper of Prudence, the youngest sister, now Mrs. Todd, paled into insignificance beside that of the others, but it was a very pretty thing in tempers nevertheless, and would have been thought remarkable in any other family in Scarboro.

You may have noted the fact that it is a person's virtues as often as his vices that make him difficult to live with. Mrs. Todd's masterfulness and even her jealousy might have been endured, by the aid of fasting and prayer, but her neatness, her economy, and her forehandedness made a combination that only the grace of God could have abided with comfortably, so that Jerry Todd's comparative success is a matter of local tradition. Punctuality is a praiseworthy virtue enough, but as the years went on, Mrs. Todd blew her breakfast horn at so early an hour that the neighbors were in some doubt as to whether it might not herald the supper of the day before. They also predicted that she would have her funeral before she was fairly dead, and related with great gusto that when she heard there was to be an eclipse of the sun on Monday, the 26th of July, she wished they could have it the 25th, as Sunday would be so much more convenient than wash-day.

She had oilcloth on her kitchen to save the floor, and oilcloth mats to save the oilcloth; yet Jerry's boots had to be taken off in the shed, and he was required to walk through in his stocking feet. She blackened her stove three times a day, washed her dishes in the woodhouse, in order to keep her sink clean, and kept one pair of blinds open in the sitting-room, but spread newspapers over the carpet wherever the sun shone in.

It was the desire of Jerry's heart to give up the fatigues and exposures of stage-driving, and "keep store," but Mrs. Todd deemed it much better for him to be in the open air than dealing out rum and molasses to a roystering crew. This being her view of the case, it is unnecessary to state that he went on driving the stage.

"Do you wear a flannel shirt, Jerry?" asked Pel Frost once. "I don' know," he replied, "ask Mis' Todd; she keeps the books."

"Women-folks" (he used to say to a casual passenger), "like all other animiles, has to be trained up before they're real good comp'ny. You have to begin with 'em early, and begin as you mean to hold out. When they once git in the habit of takin' the bit in their teeth and runnin', it's too late for you to hold 'em in."

It was only to strangers that he aired his convictions on the training of "womenfolks," though for that matter he might safely have done it even at home; for everybody in Limington knew that it would always have been too late to begin with the Widder Bixby, since, like all the Stovers of Scarboro, she had been born with the bit in her teeth. Jerry had never done anything he wanted to since he had married her, and he hadn't really wanted to do that. He had been rather candid with her on this point (as candid as a tenderhearted and obliging man can be with a woman who is determined to marry him, and has two good reasons why she should to every one of his why he shouldn't), and this may have been the reason for her jealousy. Although by her superior force she had overborne his visible reluctance, she, being a woman, or at all events of the female gender, could never quite forget that she had done the wooing.

Certainly his charms were not of the sort to tempt women from the strict and narrow path, yet the fact remained that the Widder Bixby was jealous, and more than one person in Limington was aware of it.

Pelatiah, otherwise "Pel" Frost, knew more about the matter than most other folks, because he had unlimited time to devote to general culture. Though not yet thirty years old, he was the laziest man in York County. (Jabe Slocum had not then established his record; and Jot Bascom had ruined his by cutting his hay before it was dead in the summer of '49, always alluded to afterwards in Pleasant River as the year when gold was discovered and Jot Bascom cut his hay.)

Pel was a general favorite in half a dozen villages, where he was the life of the loafers' bench. An energetic loafer can attend properly to one bench, but it takes genius as well as assiduity to do justice to six of them. His habits were decidedly convivial, and he spent a good deal of time at the general musters, drinking and carousing with the other ne'er-do-weels. You may be sure he was no favorite of Mrs. Todd's; and she represented to him all that is most undesirable in womankind, his taste running decidedly to rosy, smiling, easygoing ones who had no regular hours for meals, but could have a dinner on the table any time in fifteen minutes after you got there.

Now, a certain lady with a noticeable green frock and a white "drawn-in" cape bonnet had graced the Midnight Cry on its journey from Limington to Saco on three occasions during the month of July. Report said that she was a stranger who had appeared at the post-office in a wagon driven by a small, freckled boy.

The first trip passed without comment; the second provoked some discussion; on the occasion of the third, Mrs. Todd said nothing, because there seemed nothing to say, but she felt so out-of-sorts that she cut Jerry's hair close to his head, though he particularly fancied the thin fringe of curls at the nape of his neck.

Pel Frost went over to Todd's one morning to borrow an axe, and seized a favorable opportunity to ask casually, "Oh, Mis' Todd, did Jerry find out the name o' that woman in a green dress and white bunnit that rid to Saco with him last week?"

"Mr. Todd's got something better to do than get acquainted with his lady passengers," snapped Mrs. Todd, "'specially as they always ride inside."

"I know they gen'ally do," said Pel, shouldering the axe (it was for his mother's use), "but this one rides up in front part o' the way, so I thought mebbe Jerry 'd find out something 'bout her. She's han'some as a picture, but she must have a good strong back to make the trip down 'n' up in one day."

Nothing could have been more effective or more effectual than this blow dealt with consummate skill. Having thus driven the iron into Mrs. Todd's soul, Pel entertained his mother with an account of the interview while she chopped the kindling-wood. He had no special end in view when, Iago-like, he dropped his first poisoned seed in Mrs. Todd's fertile mind, or, at most, nothing worse than the hope that matters might reach an unendurable point, and Jerry might strike for his altars and his fires. Jerry was a man and a brother, and petticoat government must be discouraged whenever and wherever possible, or the world would soon cease to be a safe place to live in. Pel's idea grew upon him in the night watches, and the next morning he searched his mother's garret till he found a green dress and a white bonnet. Putting them in a basket, he walked out on the road a little distance till he met the stage, when, finding no passengers inside, he asked Jerry to let him jump in and "ride a piece." Once within, he hastily donned the green wrapper and tell-tale headgear, and, when the Midnight Cry rattled down the stony hill past the Todd house, Pel took good care to expose a large green sleeve and the side of a white bonnet at the stage window. It was easy enough to cram the things back into the basket, jump out, and call a cordial thank you to the unsuspecting Jerry. He was rewarded for his ingenuity and enterprise at night, when he returned Mrs. Todd's axe, for just as he reached the back door he distinctly heard her say that if she saw that green woman on the stage again, she would knock her off with a broomstick as sure as she was a Stover of Scarboro. As a matter of fact she was equal to it. Her great-grandmother had been born on a soil where the broomstick is a prominent factor in settling connubial differences; and if it occurred to her at this juncture, it is a satisfactory proof of the theory of atavism.

Pel intended to see this domestic tragedy through to the end, and accordingly took another brief trip in costume the very next week, hoping to be the witness of a scene of blood and carnage. But Mrs. Todd did not stir from her house, although he was confident she had seen "my lady green-sleeves" from her post at the window. Puzzled by her apathy, and much disappointed in her temper, he took off the dress, and, climbing up in front, rode to Moderation, where he received an urgent invitation to go over to the county fair at Gorham. The last idea was always the most captivating to Pel, and he departed serenely for a stay of several days without so much luggage as a hairbrush. His mother's best clothespin basket, to say nothing of its contents, appeared at this juncture to be an unexpected incumbrance; so on the spur of the moment he handed it up to Jerry just as the stage was starting, saying, "If Mis' Todd has a brash to-night, you can clear yourself by showing her this basket, but for massy sakes don't lay it on to me! You can stan' it better'n I can,—you 're more used to it!"

Jerry took the basket, and when he was well out on the road he looked inside and saw a bright green calico wrapper, a white cape bonnet, a white "fall veil," and a pair of white cotton gloves. He had ample time for reflection, for it was a hot day, and though he drove slowly, the horses were sweating at every pore. Pel Frost, then, must have overheard his wife's storm of reproaches, perhaps even her threats of violence. It had come to this, that he was the village laughing-stock, a butt of ridicule at the store and tavern.

Now, two years before this, Jerry Todd had for the first and only time in his married life "put his foot down." Mrs. Todd had insisted on making him a suit of clothes much against his wishes. When finished she put them on him almost by main force, though his plaintive appeals would have melted any but a Stover-of-Scarboro heart. The stuff was a large plaid, the elbows and knees came in the wrong places, the seat was lined with enameled cloth, and the sleeves cut him in the armholes.

Mr. Todd said nothing for a moment, but the pent-up slavery of years stirred in him, and, mounting to his brain, gave him a momentary courage that resembled intoxication. He retired, took off the suit, hung it over his arm, and, stalking into the sitting-room in his undergarments, laid it on the table before his astonished spouse, and, thumping it dramatically, said firmly, "I—will—not—wear—them—clo'es!" whereupon he fell into silence again and went to bed.

The joke of the matter was, that, all unknown to himself, he had absolutely frightened Mrs. Todd. If only he could have realized the impressiveness and the thorough success of his first rebellion! But if he had realized it he could not have repeated it often, for so much virtue went out of him on that occasion that he felt hardly able to drive the stage for days afterward.

"I shall have to put down my foot agin," he said to himself on the eventful morning when Pel presented him with the basket. "Dern my luck, I've got to do it agin, when I ain't hardly got over the other time." So, after an hour's plotting and planning, he made some purchases in Biddeford and started on his return trip. He was very low in his mind, thinking, if his wife really meditated upon warfare, she was likely to inspect the stage that night, but giving her credit in his inmost heart for too much common sense to use a broomstick,—a woman with her tongue!

The Midnight Cry rattled on lumberingly. Its route had been shortened, and Mrs. Todd wanted its name changed to something less outlandish, such as the Rising Sun, or the Breaking Dawn, or the High Noon, but her idea met with no votaries; it had been, was, and ever should be, the Midnight Cry, no matter what time it set out or got back. It had seen its best days, Jerry thought, and so had he, for that matter. Yet he had been called "a likely feller" when he married the Widder Bixby, or rather when she married him. Well, the mischief was done; all that remained was to save a remnant of his self-respect, and make an occasional dash for liberty.

He did all his errands with his usual care, dropping a blue ribbon for Doxy Morton's Sunday hat, four cents' worth of gum-camphor for Almira Berry, a spool of cotton for Mrs. Wentworth, and a pair of "galluses" for Living Bean. He finally turned into the "back-nippin'" road from Bonny Eagle to Limington, and when he was within forty rods of his own house he stopped to water his horses. If he feared a scene he had good reason, for as the horses climbed the crest of the long hill the lady in green was by his side on the box. He looked anxiously ahead, and there, in a hedge of young alder bushes, he saw something stirring, and, unless he was greatly mistaken, a birch broom lay on the ground near the hedge.

Notwithstanding these danger signals, Jerry's arm encircled the plump waist of the lady in green, and, emboldened by the shades of twilight, his lips sought the identical spot under the white "fall veil" where her incendiary mouth might be supposed to lurk, quite "fit for treasons, stratagems, and spoils." This done, he put on the brake and headed his horses toward the fence. He was none too soon, for the Widder Bixby, broom in hand, darted out from the alders and approached the stage with objurgations which, had she rated them at their proper value, needed no supplement in the way of blows. Jerry gave one terror-stricken look, wound his reins round the whipstock, and, leaping from his seat, disappeared behind a convenient tree.

At this moment of blind rage Mrs. Todd would have preferred to chastise both her victims at once; but, being robbed of one by Jerry's cowardly flight, her weapon descended upon the other with double force. There was no lack of courage here at least. Whether the lady in green was borne up by the consciousness of virtue, whether she was too proud to retreat, or whatever may have been her animating reason, the blow fell, yet she stood her ground and gave no answering shriek. Enraged as much by her rival's cool resistance as by her own sense of injury, the Widder Bixby aimed full at the bonnet beneath which were the charms that had befuddled Jerry Todd's brain. To blast the fatal beauty that had captivated her wedded husband was the Widder

Bixby's idea, and the broom descended. A shower of seeds and pulp, a copious spattering of pumpkin juice, and the lady in green fell resistlessly into her assailant's arms; her straw body, her wooden arms and pumpkin head, decorating the earth at her feet! Mrs. Todd stared helplessly at the wreck she had made, not altogether comprehending the ruse that had led to her discomfiture, but fully conscious that her empire was shaken to its foundations. She glanced in every direction, and then hurling the hateful green-and-white livery into the stage, she gathered up all traces of the shameful fray, and sweeping them into her gingham apron ran into the house in a storm of tears and baffled rage.

Jerry stayed behind the tree for some minutes, and when the coast was clear he mounted the seat and drove to the store and the stable. When he had put up his horses he went into the shed, took off his boots as usual, but, despite all his philosophy, broke into a cold sweat of terror as he crossed the kitchen threshold. "I can't stand many more of these times when I put my foot down," he thought, "they're too weakening!"

But he need not have feared. There was a good supper under the mosquito netting on the table, and, most unusual luxury, a pot of hot tea. Mrs. Todd had gone to bed and left him a pot of tea!

Which was the more eloquent apology!

Jerry never referred to the lady in green, then or afterwards; he was willing to let well enough alone; but whenever his spouse passed a certain line, which, being a Stover of Scarboro, she was likely to do about once in six months, he had only to summon his recreant courage and glance meaningly behind the kitchen door, where the birch broom hung on a nail. It was a simple remedy to outward appearances, but made his declining years more comfortable. I can hardly believe that he ever took Pel Frost into his confidence, but Pel certainly was never more interesting to the loafers' bench than when he told the story of the eventful trip of the Midnight Cry and "the breaking in of the Widder Bixby."

NOTES: 1. On page 20, reentered is spelled with diaeresis over the second "e".

2. On pages 153 & 154 the verses beginning respectively "Rebel mourner" and "This gro-o-oanin' world" are accompanied with staves of music in the treble clef.

Milton Keynes UK
Ingram Content Group UK Ltd.
UKHW030911151124
451262UK00006B/825